The Fou

The Foundation Pit

Andrey Platonov

Translated and with an introduction by
Mirra Ginsburg

NORTHWESTERN UNIVERSITY PRESS
EVANSTON, ILLINOIS

Northwestern University Press
Evanston, Illinois 60208-4170

10 9 8 7 6 5

Printed in the United States of America

ISBN 0-8101-1145-4

Library of Congress Cataloging-in-Publication Data

Platonov, Andrei Platonovich, 1899–1951.
    [Kotlovan. English]
    The foundation pit / Andrey Platonov ; translated by Mirra
Ginsburg.
        p.   cm. — (European classics)
    ISBN 0-8101-1145-4 (alk. paper)
    I. Ginsburg, Mirra. II. Title. III. Series: European classics
(Evanston, Ill.)
    PG3476.P543K613   1994
    891.73´42—DC20   93–49836
                                                      CIP

Translator's Introduction

"Beauty," wrote Platonov, "does not exist separately, by itself. It is the property of all . . . beauty is all days, and all things." He also wrote, "We grow out of the earth, out of all its impurities, and everything that is on earth is also in us."[1]

Andrey Platonov, a unique and extraordinary writer, came into Russian literature in the 1920s, at a time when it abounded in unique and extraordinary talents. Like the others in that brilliant array—Zamyatin, Bulgakov, Babel, Pilnyak, Olesha, Zoshchenko, all of them silenced or destroyed at the height of their powers—he became a victim of his time, one more example of the vicissitudes of literature under dictatorship. Yet his fate, like his talent and his origins, followed a pattern of its own.

Less spectacular than the others, less flashing, more muted, he was also less European, less worldly, more Russian. His origins were not in a cosmopolitan and intellectual middle-class milieu, but in a world of urban working people, of artisans just recently emerged from the peasantry.

The locale of most of his stories was his native province of Voronezh, in the black earth belt some two hundred miles south of Moscow, where he was born in 1899, the eldest son of a railway mechanic. At the age of thirteen, Platonov went to work to help his father support what was by then a family of ten. He worked in many places at many trades. Nevertheless, after the Revolution and service in the Red Army, he continued his schooling and graduated in 1924 from the Voronezh Polytechnical Institute with a degree in electrical engineering. He worked in the field of electrification and land reclamation in various provinces in central Russia. Here he became thoroughly familiar with the devastated post-Revolutionary village and the peasants—their life, their attitudes, their speech.

Throughout these years he contributed poems, stories, and articles to a number of local newspapers. In 1927 he went to Moscow and soon devoted himself entirely to literary work. A late arrival, he missed much of the rich and varied flowering of early Soviet literature. He came in time to witness the beginning of its ruthless extermination. The RAPP (Russian Association of Proletarian Writers) and its notorious leader Leopold Averbakh were just about to be entrusted with the destruction of everything original and alive, and very soon Platonov himself became their target.

For a time, Platonov was close to the Pereval group, which consisted of peasant and working class writers, as well as fellow travelers, and advocated service to the revolution while preserving the earlier cultural and literary values and creative freedom. On the whole, however, he never became "acculturated" in the literary world of the capital, but remained a solitary figure, going his own way—in his subject matter, his characters, his language, his style, his own brand of irony, his own humor, and his own sadness.

His work did not fit into any "mainstream." And, although he was a Communist, and had ardently welcomed the revolution and what he saw as its promise, his Communism was closer to early Christianity than to the brutal state religion that was being forcibly imposed on Russia.

His first collection of stories, *The Locks of Epiphany* (1927), won him instant recognition as a major writer. The title story, however, set in the time of the violent reforms and often impossible projects of Peter the Great, at the cost of thousands of lives, clearly mirrored the present and betrayed his emerging doubts.

Distrusted and under attack almost from the very first, he was accused of a bevy of sins: pessimism, anarchism, nihilism, antirealism, symbolism, petty-bourgeois and kulak psychology, failure to understand the larger purposes of Communist construction which justified the sacrifice of the individual, hostile mockery of the Revolution, and even Trotskyist deviations.

Barred from book publication for long periods, he was reduced to virtual nonbeing as a writer through most of his lifetime, earning a bare living as a book reviewer writing under several pen names. The stretches of enforced silence as an artist were punctuated by the occasional appearance of a story in a magazine or a slender collection, usually followed by renewed outbursts from party critics. Indeed, except for the periods when he was subject to intense vilification, his name and his work were almost unknown to Russian readers.

Despite the hostile atmosphere, Platonov continued writing in his own manner, which obstinately refused to fit into the requisite forms and requisite moods. He remained a Communist, but he held up his early Communist vision—the vision expressed in the simplest terms by many of his characters—to the realities of the time, and clearly found them wanting. The satirical vein in his writing manifested itself most strongly in the late 1920s and early 1930s, the crucial years of the First Five-Year Plan and the ruthless collectivization of agriculture, as well as the sharp tightening of control over art and literature.

His two major works, *Chevengur* and *The Foundation Pit*, were written during this period. *Chevengur*, a rich novel of the absurd set in the early post-Revolutionary years, took four years in the writing (1926–29). Its opening chapter, "The Origin of the Master," appeared in *Krasnaya Nov'* in 1928. The rest, when reputedly already in type, was banned at the last moment.

Platonov, dismayed, appealed to the authorities to no avail. Gorky, whom he asked to intervene, replied evasively, "The censors will not pass it." *The Foundation Pit*, a considerably shorter work reflecting the grim present, was written in four months (December 1929–April 1930). Both novels remained in manuscript for many decades.

Two shorter satirical works appeared in magazines (evidently through the editors' oversight), with disastrous results for the author.

In the story "Doubting Makar," published in 1929 in the magazine *Oktyabr*, Platonov's hero falls asleep, "and his suffering passed into a dream: in the dream he saw a mountain or some elevation, and on the mountain stood a man of science . . . the man stood silently, without seeing the grieving Makar and thinking only about the general scale of things, not about the private Makar. The face of that most learned man was lit by the glow of faraway mass life spreading in the distance beneath him, and his eyes were terrible and dead from being on such a height and looking too far."

The story provoked a vitriolic reply by Averbakh, replete with charges of antisocial individualism, anticollectivisim, pseudo-humanism, nihilism, kulak deviations and anarchic hostility to the Soviet state.

In 1934, the *Literary Encyclopedia* wrote that Platonov showed "the Soviet state apparatus not as a form of the participation of workers and peasants in governing the country, but as a mechanical apparatus of coercion, of the leveling down of the individual. Objectively, Platonov's story ["Doubting Makar"— *tr.*] reinforced the Trotskyist attack on the party and on proletarian dictatorship."

Another satire, "Vprok" (For the Future Good), published in *Krasnaya Nov'* in 1931, was met with renewed attacks. An oddly ambiguous work, written in the form of a rather motley reportage by a simple-minded well-wisher who sets out to observe the progress of the collectivization, it is a many-faceted critique. At times using praise so excessive that it borders on mockery, it reveals, as though unwittingly, the poverty, backwardness and ignorance of the Russian village, and the endless confusion, abuses and absurdities attending the efforts both of those who favored collectivization and those who sought to foil it. All this, with superb wit, sorrow, and great warmth for the Russian peasant.

"Vprok," like "Doubting Makar," evoked Stalin's displeasure, and the journal's frightened editor, Alexander Fadeev, denounced Platonov in a particularly dangerous and vicious diatribe, calling him a "kulak agent" and branding the story a "kulak sortie." An almost total ban was imposed at the time on further publication of Platonov's works.

The appearance in 1937, during a short-lived reprieve, of a small collection of stories (the only one between 1929 and 1942), was followed by the usual chorus of abuse, this time for his "obsession with suffering" when the country needed "positive and optimistic works."

Platonov escaped prosecution during the purges of the 1930s, but in 1938 his only son, a boy of fifteen, was arrested—for alleged plotting—and sent to a labor camp. All efforts to obtain the boy's release were unavailing until 1940 when he came home, dying of tuberculosis. Platonov nursed him through his last illness, contracting the disease himself.

When World War II broke out, he volunteered to serve as a war correspondent. He reported from various fronts and published a number of stories in periodicals, simple in style and devoted chiefly to wartime themes. These were collected into several small books, both for adults and for children.

He returned from the war a desperately sick man. The final blow came with the publication of the warm and tender story, "Homecoming," in *Novy Mir* (1946), dealing with the problems of life behind the lines in wartime and the difficult adjustment of a returned soldier. It was greeted with a new outburst of vilification. Incredibly, the story was attacked for "maligning" the

Soviet family and the Soviet soldier. This marked the virtual end of Platonov as a writer. All he was able to publish after that (with the help of friends) were occasional book reviews, again under pen names, some pieces in children's magazines, and two collections of splendidly retold folktales, Bashkir and Russian. He died in 1951, after years of poverty and illness, leaving a large body of unpublished writings including his greatest works, *The Foundation Pit* and *Chevengur*.

◆　◆　◆

Platonov's posthumous "rehabilitation" and, indeed, discovery began (cautiously) in 1958, with the publication of a small collection of stories, followed during the ensuing decades by other volumes, consisting chiefly of reprints from various journals and earlier collections. His work was widely hailed in the Soviet Union, both by the faithful and by dissidents. However, the authors of the introductions to his books, as well as many Soviet critics, assiduously tried to place him into the framework of the usual clichés, seeking to show that, despite some errors, he was really "one of us."

The satirical stories, even those published while he lived, were at first largely avoided, not to speak of his longer works, which remained in manuscript. These eventually found their way into Samizdat and to publication abroad. *The Foundation Pit* first appeared in the emigre journal *Grani* in Germany in 1968. *Chevengur* was published in book form (in an incomplete version) in 1972 by the YMCA Press in France. They had to wait for publication in their homeland until the late 1980s: *The Foundation Pit* in *Novy Mir* in 1987, *Chevengur* in *Druzhba Narodov* in 1988. Numerous book publications followed.

Platonov soon became an object of great—at times almost religious—veneration, this time with readers of various political and philosophical persuasions claiming him as "ours."

Today, his stories, novels, and plays are published again and again in editions of hundreds of thousands. Translations and studies of his works are also widely published abroad. After a lifetime of rejection and persecution, of near anonymity, Platonov has emerged as one of the great masters of twentieth-century Russian and world literature—an artist of profound genius, modesty, and courage, and, in his art, absolute integrity and clarity of vision.

◆   ◆   ◆

Both in style and in content, Platonov's best works, created in the short span of a little over a decade, fall into two distinct yet, in his case, closely related categories—lyric and satirical. Most of his stories, illuminating individual relationships, belong to the former. His longer works and the stories in which he examines the social events of the time are satirical tragedies, told with great compassion and with grief over the unredeemed costs in human suffering.

The dominant quality in Platonov's work is compassion. Not the violent, frenzied compassion of Dostoevsky, but muted, sorrowing, almost resigned, almost hopeless. Like Voshchev, one of the central characters of *The Foundation Pit*, he collected in his stories "all the poor, rejected objects, all the small, unknown, forgotten things."

"Everything," he wrote, "lives and suffers in the world, without understanding or knowledge."

Platonov not only stressed the tragic humanity of man, he humanized inert, inanimate things at a time when man himself was being dehumanized, reduced to a will-less automaton in the service of the Communist abstraction and the state machine. Amid the violence, the brutality of "a new society in the building," Platonov was like the holy fool of old who spoke the simple truths that were as dangerous to the new rulers as they had been to the bloody tsars of early Russia.

Life in his works has a naked quality. His characters suffer defenselessly as if unprotected by a single layer of skin, a single one of the ordinary devices in which people take refuge from the pain of living. In its intolerable clarity of vision, his writing could be almost that of a "naïf," were it not for the careful and conscious artistry that went into its making. In discussing Pushkin's *The Bronze Horseman*, Platonov wrote in 1937 that the poet "resolved its true themes not logically, by the method of plot development, but by the method of a 'second meaning,' where resolution is achieved not by the action of the poem's characters, but by the entire music, the organization of the work—an added force which also creates in the reader's mind the image of the author as the principal hero of the work."[2] This might equally well define Platonov's method, especially in works like *The Foundation Pit*.

In Russian literature there is an extraordinary continuity of tradition. Indeed, continuity may not be quite the right word: the past is constantly and powerfully present. Pushkin, Gogol, Tolstoy, Dostoevsky are not, like their American or even English counterparts, writers who lived and wrote in a remote and long-vanished past. They continue to be vital, undimmed presences, contemporaries, a living part of the awareness of every literate Russian. In major, significant literature, the thread is unbroken, and virtually every writer of talent and substance has worked in close communication with those who have gone before.

The giants themselves have been aware of this. Dostoevsky is quoted as saying, "We have all come out of Gogol's 'Overcoat.'"

There has also been an unbroken continuum of concerns and ideas. One of the important facets of Dostoevsky's *Notes from Underground* was his debate with the idea of the Crystal Palace in Chernyshevsky's *What Is to Be Done*, a symbol of man's capacity to build an ideal society based on reason and good will. Zamyatin's *We* is a bitterly satirical picture of the Crystal Palace achieved. Olesha's *Envy* takes up another aspect of the problem (again, a variation on the *Notes from Underground*)—the place of the nonconforming, non-active, contemplative individual who refuses to be seduced by material benefits.

The pivotal figures and the pivotal questions form an unbroken chain, and even the mutilations of the Soviet period had merely driven the fundamental concerns of Russian literature underground. Thus—Zamyatin, Bulgakov, Pasternak, much of Platonov, Solzhenitsyn, as well as many lesser figures.

For all its originality and uniqueness of style and perception, *The Foundation Pit* is integrally bound with this tradition. It is in a direct line of descent from the *Notes from Underground* and *We*. It too examines the costs and the value of the building of a splendid "general" house where people will live happily and "in silence." It too is concerned with man's intention and achievement, man's goals, internal and external, man's power over his destiny and the price to be paid for the effort to bend life to man's will.

"Don't people decrease in their sense of life when buildings increase?" asks Voshchev. "Man will make a building and unmake himself. Who will live in it then?"

The Foundation Pit is many things. It is a cautionary tale, a philosophic inquiry, a political grotesque, a symbolic portrait of a society and a period, and a fragmented self-portrait—a work of many facets and marvelous inventiveness. Its characters, like those in many of Platonov's tales, are waifs, lost, lonely, abstracted, displaced in geography, in society, in time, oddly lacking in "normal" human relationships. The acutely realized concreteness of their surroundings is in itself an abstraction and creates a surrealist landscape—a landscape of myth or nightmare. Through abstraction, Platonov achieves universality. Every man becomes Everyman or a facet of Everyman, and the novel assumes a larger than life, almost legendary quality.

Mirroring the cruel shambles to which revolution and human will (in all its complexities and motivations) have reduced life, Platonov brings the action, the characters, and the language itself down to ultimate absurdity. He carries *The Foundation Pit* beyond irony, beyond satire, to a point where everything becomes a tragic parody of itself.

He plays, almost musically, endless variations on character, needs, goals, and situations within this central theme of the absurd. We see Voshchev, who cannot rest until he finds the "truth of life"; the engineer Prushevsky, the "intellectual," the man who knows only "parts of dead things," who feels lost and unrelated to mankind, who longs for the fleeting glimpse of beauty and possible happiness he had in his youth and who, like Voshchev, suffers from the need to understand "meaning" in the midst of chaos; Chiklin, whose body needs to work, who breaks the ground "abolishing the ancient natural order without ability to understand it," who, like Prushevsky, suffers from a sense of loss and longing for the love which he rejected in his youth; the bullying "cripple of imperialism" Zhachev, who deals out brutal justice; bureaucratic figures like Pashkin, both preposterous and pathetic in his self-importance and his fear of those above and below; Kozlov, the stickler for the "correct" line, dying of tuberculosis, but forever denouncing improprieties to the authorities; the activist, striving to follow the party line and ending up rejected as a "leftist-rightist opportunist" and enemy of the proletariat; the neglected and starved collectivized horses who collectively forage for food and collectively eat it; the bear who is a union member. And finally, the child— one of Platonov's many unforgettable portraits of children— almost a dream child this time, a daughter of the dead, once lovely, "bourgeois" girl who had presumably crossed the paths of both Prushevsky and Chiklin; the child who represents the "bright Communist future" for whose sake all the present activity is carried on, who learns and mouths revolutionary slogans until they sound like cruel taunts, and who, in the sorrowfully ironic climax of the book, dies as winter sets in, after a macabre celebration of the floating of the "kulaks" in a raft downriver to the sea and the victorious establishment of the "collective farm."

As always, Platonov's sorrow and compassion extend equally to everything—man, animal, used-up, discarded things. And the whole world is ultimately seen as a shattered, used-up, discarded thing.

The novel abounds in multilevel, multifaceted allusions, some of them, referring to its time and place, clear only to Russians, others apparent to the discerning eye of any reader.

One of the many extraordinary aspects of *The Foundation Pit* is its style. Its language is that of speech, not of "written literature." In this it is related to the works of Leskov, Remizov, Zoshchenko, and Zamyatin, who taught that not only the dialogue but also the narrative of a story should be true to the language of its characters and milieu. The works of Zoshchenko and Platonov are particularly vivid examples of this.

Zoshchenko made use of the "new" language of the half-literate urban proletariat which resulted from the Revolutionary upheaval—a combination of folk speech and the language of the intellectuals, with a heavy admixture of current political and bureaucratic jargon taken over by the people and misused in grotesque ways. Zoshchenko's language is a commentary on the state of the culture. It is the language of (bitter) comedy.

Platonov, in his satirical works, based his style on the speech of the largely unschooled workers and peasants of the Russian province, which still bore echoes at that time of the stately rhythms of folklore and the Slavonic of church rituals. He avoided the foreign accretions in the language of the educated classes, and confined himself to the indigenous Russian of his characters. With this "simplified" vocabulary, and the inevitable (paradoxical and tragicomic) political jargon of the day, he fashioned his own inimitable language that achieved miracles of expressiveness and power.

But the style of *The Foundation Pit* is not merely a reflection of the dislocations in the social life of the country, and not merely an echoing of the absurdities and transformations in the people's speech. It is the conscious and deliberate construction of a sensitive artist. Through incongruity of verbal choices and juxtapositions, Platonov expanded the limits of meaning and lent words new and unexpected dimensions. The deformation of syntax and the strangeness of usage are not a striving for effect, but a striving for absolute veracity to the writer's vision and experience.

◆　　◆　　◆

In conclusion, a note on the translation. Ideally, the translator should achieve the closest verbal fidelity possible in another language, as well as the closest approximation to the rhythm, tone, nuance, form, and mood of the original. The ideal is a virtually impossible one, since the experience, social and individual, the associations, the very values and responses to facts, words, ideas, colors, and tonalities are hopelessly different in different cultures. Yet the ideal remains and we struggle to come as close to it as we can. This is further complicated by the fact that each individual work requires its own specific approach.

An author's "eccentric" use of language renders verbal fidelity especially problematic. To avoid the danger of obscuring or violating the total impact of the work, we must try to find solutions that will do justice both to the style and to the author's intent. *The Foundation Pit* makes enormous demands on the translator in this respect.

And finally, if the reader finds much of the text un-English it is because the original is un-Russian. Indeed, if I have sinned occasionally, it was in the opposite direction—reverting some of the "un-meaning" to meaning, especially where the verbal and formal distortions reflect specific Russian conditions of the time, which are without equivalents in American or English experience—so that the reader unfamiliar with the period and place and references would be able to find his way and receive as much of the statement as could be conveyed without violating the work's integrity. And the statement itself is as timely today as it was when the novel was written.

MIRRA GINSBURG
1994

NOTES

1. From the Introduction to *The Blue Deep*, a collection of his poems (1922).
2. In "Pushkin, Our Comrade," *Literaturny Kritik*, January, 1937.

The Foundation Pit

On the day when he reached the thirtieth year of his personal life Voshchev was discharged from the small machine factory where he had earned the means of his existence. The dismissal notice stated that he was being separated from his job because of his increasing loss of powers and tendency to stop and think amidst the general flow of work.

Back in his room, Voshchev gathered his belongings into a sack and went out, to gain a better understanding of his future in the open air. But the air was empty; the motionless trees carefully held the heat in their leaves; and dust lay dully on the empty road. Such was the situation in nature. Voshchev could not make up his mind where he was drawn. At the edge of town, he leaned his elbows on the low fence of an estate where homeless children were trained for work and a useful life. Beyond that the town ended. There was only a tavern for migrant laborers and workers in low-paid trades, which stood without yard or garden, like an institution. And after the tavern there was a clay hill, with an old tree growing on it, alone in the bright weather. Voshchev walked to the tavern and entered, hearing sincere human voices.

Inside, there were intemperate men, abandoning themselves to forgetfulness of their troubles, and Voshchev was saddened, but he also felt easier among them. He stayed in the tavern till evening, until a rushing wind blew up with a change of weather. Voshchev went to the open window to watch the coming of the night, and saw the tree on the clay hill: it swayed in the wind, its leaves curling with secret shame. Somewhere, perhaps in the Soviet Trade Workers' Park, a band was droning wearily; monotonous sounds that never quite turned into music were carried into nature by the wind across the barren land next to the ravine. The wind was followed once more by silence, then by still deeper, soundless dusk. Voshchev sat down by the window to observe the tender darkness of the night, to listen to a variety of melancholy sounds, and suffer the anguish of his heart, encased in stonelike, rigid bones.

"Hey, waiter!" someone shouted in the now silent room. "Bring us a couple of mugs, to wet the gullet!"

Voshchev had long ago discovered that people always came to taverns in pairs, like a bride and groom, and sometimes in entire friendly wedding parties.

This time the waiter did not serve the beer, and the two roofers who had just come in wiped their thirsty lips with their aprons.

"Bureaucrat! A working man should get his orders filled at the flick of a thumb, and you turn up your nose!"

But the waiter would not waste his strength at work; he saved it for his private life, and never entered into arguments.

"The establishment is closed, citizens. Go and find something to do at home."

The roofers took a salt cracker each from a saucer, put them in their mouths, and walked out. Voshchev remained alone in the tavern.

"Citizen! You ordered one mug, and then you sit there like a lifetime fixture. You paid for the drink, not the premises!"

Voshchev picked up his sack and went out into the night. The questioning sky glowed over him with the tormenting power of its stars, but in town the lights were already out.

4

People who could sleep, slept, having filled themselves with supper. Voshchev stepped down over the crumbling earth into the ravine and stretched out on his stomach, to fall asleep and get away from himself. But sleep requires peace of mind, faith in life, forgiveness for suffering endured, and Voshchev lay in arid tension of wakefulness and did not know—was he of any use in the world, or could everything go on just as well without him? A wind came up from places unknown, so that people would not suffocate, and somewhere on the outskirts a dog announced in a feeble, doubtful voice that it was on duty.

"The dog is sad, it lives only because it was born, the same as me."

Voshchev's body turned pale with weariness; his eyelids felt cold, and he closed them over his warm eyes.

The tavernkeeper was readying his establishment, winds and grasses swayed around Voshchev in the sun when he reluctantly opened his eyes, filled with renewed moist strength. He had to live and eat again; therefore he went to see the trade union committee, to defend his unneeded labor.

"The management says that you were standing and thinking in the middle of production," they told him at the trade union committee. "What were you thinking about, Comrade Voshchev?"

"About the plan of life."

"The factory works according to the plan laid down by the Trust. As for your private life, you could plan it out at the club or in the Red Reading Room."

"I was thinking about the general plan of life. I'm not worried about my own life, that's no secret to me."

"And what could you accomplish?"

"I could have thought up something like happiness, and spiritual meaning would improve productivity."

"Happiness will come from materialism, Comrade Voshchev, and not from meaning. We cannot defend you, you are a politically ignorant man, and we don't wish to find ourselves at the tail end of the masses."

Voshchev wanted to ask for some other work, even the feeblest, just so that he would earn enough to eat; and he would do his thinking on his own time. But how can one ask for anything if there's no respect for a man, and Voshchev saw that those people had no feeling for him.

"You're scared of being at the tail end of the masses; naturally, a tail's the hind extremity. So you've climbed up on their necks."

"The government gave you an extra hour for your thinking, Voshchev. You used to work eight hours, and now it's only seven. You should have lived and kept quiet! If everybody starts thinking all at once, who'll do the acting?"

"Without thought, there won't be any sense in the action," Voshchev said reflectively.

He left the trade union committee without getting help. The path before him lay in the heat of summer. On either side people were building technical improvements and houses where the masses, homeless until now, would live in silence. Voshchev's body was indifferent to comforts. He could live in the open without exhaustion; he had been tormented with unhappiness when he had had enough to eat, when he had rest and quiet in his old room. He passed the tavern outside of town once more and looked again at the place where he had spent the night. Something of his life remained there, and Voshchev found himself in space, with nothing but the horizon before him and the feeling of the wind on his bowed face.

A mile away stood the house of the road overseer. Accustomed to emptiness around, the overseer quarreled loudly with his wife, and the woman sat at the open window with her child in her lap and answered her husband with shouts of abuse. The child sat silently and tugged at the ruffle of his shirt, understanding, but saying nothing.

The child's patience cheered Voshchev up. He saw that the mother and father had no sense of the meaning of life

6

and were angry, but the child lived without reproach, growing up into his own sorrows. Voshchev decided to strain his soul and put his mind to work without sparing his body, in order to return soon to the house of the overseer of the road and tell the comprehending child the secret of life, which was continually being forgotten by his parents. Their bodies are just moving mechanically, Voshchev thought, observing the parents. They have no feeling for the essence of things.

"How come you don't feel the essence of things?" Voshchev asked, turning to the window. "You have a living child, and you are quarreling. And he was born to complete the whole world!"

The husband and wife looked at the witness with fear of conscience, hidden behind the malice of their faces.

"If you have no way of living peacefully, respect your child—it will be better for you."

"And what do you want here?" the road overseer asked in a thin, angry voice. "You're on your way, keep going. That's what the road was paved for. . . ."

Voshchev stood hesitating in the middle of the road. The family waited for him to go and kept its malice in reserve.

"I'd go, but I have no place to go to. Is it far to another town?"

"Not far," said the overseer. "If you don't stand around, the road will bring you there."

"And you, honor your child," said Voshchev. "When you die, he will live."

After these words, Voshchev walked about a mile from the overseer's house and sat down at the edge of a ditch. He began to feel doubts concerning his life and the weakness of his body without truth. He could no longer strive and walk along the road without knowing the exact construction of the whole world and what a man must seek in it. Wearied by thought, he lay down in the dusty roadside grass. It was hot; the daytime wind was blowing, roosters crowed somewhere in a village. Everything surrendered

7

itself to meek, unquestioning existence, Voshchev alone was apart and silent. A dead, fallen leaf lay near his head, brought by the wind from some distant tree; now this leaf was destined to find peace in the earth. Voshchev picked up the dry leaf and hid it in a secret compartment of his sack, where he collected all sorts of lost, unfortunate objects. You did not know the meaning of your life, Voshchev thought with careful sympathy. Lie here; I'll find out why you lived and died. Since nobody needs you and you are lying uselessly in the middle of things, I will keep and remember you.

"Everything lives and suffers in the world, without understanding or knowledge," said Voshchev, and got up from the roadside to go on, surrounded by general patient existence. "It's as if someone, or some few, had drawn the feeling of certainty out of us and taken it for themselves."

He walked down the road until he was exhausted. Voshchev got exhausted easily, every time his soul remembered it had ceased to know the truth.

But the town could already be seen in the distance. Its cooperative bakeries smoked, and the evening sun brightened the dust, raised higher than the housetops by the moving population. This town began with a smithy, and as Voshchev passed it a car, damaged by driving over roadless land, was being fixed there. A fat cripple stood near the hitching post and spoke to the blacksmith:

"Mish, let's have some tobacco, or I'll rip off your lock again at night!"

The blacksmith did not answer from under the car. The cripple poked him in the rear with his crutch. "Mish, you'd better quit work now. Let me have some, or I'll make trouble."

Voshchev halted near the cripple because a column of children, Young Pioneers, was coming down the street from the center of town, led by tired music.

"I gave you a whole ruble yesterday," said the blacksmith. "Can't you leave me in peace for at least a week? I'm

8

putting up and putting up with you—see I don't get fed up and burn your crutches!"

"Burn them," the cripple agreed. "The fellows will bring me in a wheelbarrow—I'll pull the roof off the smithy!"

The blacksmith was diverted by the sight of the children and, softening up, poured some tobacco into the cripple's pouch.

"Here's your plunder, you locust!"

Voshchev noticed that the cripple had no legs: one was missing altogether, and in place of the other he had a wooden attachment; he supported himself on crutches, helped along by straining the wooden extension of the amputated right leg. The cripple had no teeth at all, he had worn them clean down with chewing, but he had a huge face and a heavy stump of a body. His brown, narrow eyes observed the alien world with the greed of the deprived, with the longing of accumulated passion, and his gums worked in his mouth against each other, uttering his unheard thoughts.

The Pioneers' band, moving on, struck up the music of the youth march. Barefoot girls stepped out past the smithy in perfect time, filled with a sense of the importance of their future. Their feeble, growing bodies were dressed in sailor blouses; red berets rested lightly on their attentive, thoughtful heads; and their legs were covered with the down of childhood. Every girl, moving in the general formation, smiled with the sense of her significance, of the seriousness of her life, essential for the continuity of the formation and the power of the march. All these girl Pioneers were born at a time when the dead horses of the civil war lay in the fields, and not all of them had skin at the hour of birth, because their mothers subsisted only on the reserves of their own bodies. Therefore the face of every girl retained marks of the hardship and the weakness of her early days—meagerness of flesh and beauty of expression. But the happiness of childish friendship, the building of a future life in the play of youth and in the dignity of their stern freedom imprinted on the childish faces serious joy in place of beauty and well-fed plumpness.

Voshchev stood timidly before the eyes of the procession of these unknown, excited children. He was ashamed because the Pioneers probably knew and felt more than he did—for children are time ripening in fresh bodies, while he, Voshchev, was being shunted out by hurrying, active youth into the silence of obscurity, as life's futile attempt to attain its goal. And Voshchev felt both shame and energy. He was anxious to discover at once the universal, enduring meaning of life, in order to live ahead of the children, faster than their sunburned legs, filled with firm tenderness.

One of the girls ran out of the ranks into the rye field next to the smithy and plucked a flower. As she was bending, the little woman exposed a birthmark on her swelling body, then with the ease of imperceptible strength she flitted by, leaving a feeling of regret in two observers— Voshchev and the cripple. Voshchev glanced at the cripple: the man's face puffed out with unspent blood; he moaned and moved his hand in his pocket. Voshchev saw the feelings of the powerful maimed man, but was glad that the cripple of imperialism would never get at the socialist children. The cripple, however, watched the Pioneer procession to the end, and Voshchev became fearful for the safety and purity of the little children.

"Why don't you look with your eyes somewhere else?" he said to the legless man. "Why don't you take a smoke instead?"

"Get out of my way! Giving me orders!"

Voshchev did not move.

"You heard me!" the cripple repeated. "Or d'you want me to let you have it?"

"No," Voshchev answered. "I was afraid you'd say some word to the girl, or do something."

The cripple bowed his large head in customary anguish.

"What would I say to a child, you scum? I'm looking at

the children to remember them, because I'll die soon."

"You must have gotten hurt in the capitalist war," Voshchev said quietly. "Though old men can be cripples too, I've seen some."

The mutilated man turned his eyes to Voshchev; they were filled with the brutality of a superior mind. At first the cripple could not speak, choked with rage at the stranger. Then he said with slow bitterness:

"There are old men like that. But nobody's a cripple like you."

"I haven't been in a real war," said Voshchev. "I wouldn't have come back whole either."

"I see you haven't—that's why you're a fool! A man who hasn't been at war is like a woman who's never given birth: lives like an idiot. And I can see right through your shell!"

"Eh . . ." the blacksmith said pitifully. "I look at the children, and want to shout myself: Hurrah for May Day!"

The Pioneers' music took a rest and then struck up the march again. Voshchev continued to feel oppressed, and went on, intending to live in that town.

He walked all over town silently till evening, as if waiting for the world to make itself entirely known. But still the world remained unclear to him, and in the darkness of his body he felt a quiet spot, where there was nothing, and nothing prevented things from swaying there. Like someone living in absence from himself, Voshchev strolled past people, feeling the growing pressure of his sorrowing mind, and drawing deeper and deeper into solitude inside the cramped space of his sadness.

It was only now that he saw the center of town and the building going on there. The evening electricity had been switched on over the scaffolding, but the hushed light of the fields and the scent of wilting hay had wafted in from the general expanse outside the town and hung untouched in the air. Set apart from nature, in the bright electric place, people worked with a will, raising brick walls, carrying loads within the wooden delirium of scaffolding. Voshchev watched for a long time the erection of a tower he knew nothing about; he saw that the workmen moved smoothly, without sharp force, but something was visibly being added toward the completion of the structure.

"Don't people decrease in their sense of life when buildings increase?" Voshchev hesitated to believe. "Man will make a building and unmake himself. Who will live in it then?" Voshchev wondered as he walked away.

He left the center of town and went to the outskirts. As he walked, night fell. No people were about. Nothing but water and wind inhabited the distance of dark nature, and only birds could put into song the sorrow of this great substance, because they flew above it, and this made it easier for them.

Voshchev wandered off to a deserted spot and found himself a warm hollow for the night. Climbing down into that hole in the earth, he put under his head the sack in which he collected for remembering and avenging every obscure, neglected thing. He was saddened, and on this he fell asleep. But some man came into the field with a scythe and began to hack away at the grass thickets that had grown there from time immemorial.

By midnight the mower reached Voshchev and ordered him to get up and leave the lot.

"What lot!" Voshchev argued reluctantly. "It's just an empty place."

"And now it will be a lot. A brick building is going up here. Come and look at this place in the morning—soon it will disappear forever under the construction."

"And where shall I go?"

"You can finish sleeping in the barrack. Go there and sleep till morning, then we'll see about you."

Voshchev went where the mower told him and soon noticed a wooden barn in a former vegetable garden. Inside the barn, some seventeen or twenty people slept on their backs, and the dimmed lamp lit the unconscious human faces. All the sleepers were as thin as corpses; in each one, the narrow space between the skin and bones was occupied by veins, and the thickness of the veins showed how much blood they had to pass during the hours of strenuous labor. The cotton of the shirts conveyed exactly the slow, refreshing work of the heart, which beat close to the surface, in the darkness of the wasted body of each sleeper. Voshchev peered into the face of the sleeper nearest to him—did it express the simple happiness of a satisfied man? But the man was dead asleep, his eyes hidden deeply and sorrowfully, and his chilled legs stretched out helplessly in shabby working pants. There was no sound except of breathing in the barrack. Nobody had any dreams and nobody conversed with memories. Each man existed without any superfluity of life, and in sleep only his heart remained alive, preserving him. Voshchev felt the chill of fatigue and lay down for warmth between the bodies of two sleeping workmen. He fell asleep unknown to those people who had closed their eyes, pleased that he was spending the night beside them. And so he slept, without knowledge of the truth, until bright morning came.

In the morning some instinct struck his brain; he awakened and listened without opening his eyes.

"He's weak!"

"He is not a socially conscious man."

"It doesn't matter: capitalism made asses of our kind, and this one is a remnant of the darkness."

"If he belongs to the proper class, he'll do."

"Judging from his body, he's of the poor class."

Voshchev hesitantly opened his eyes upon the light of the new day. Yesterday's sleepers, alive, stood over him, observing his infirm condition.

"Why do you exist and walk around here?" he was asked by one, whose beard grew sparsely because he was so worn out.

"I don't exist here," said Voshchev, embarrassed that so many people had their minds on him alone at that moment. "I only think here."

"And what are you thinking for, just eating your heart out?"

"Without the truth, my body weakens, I cannot earn a living by labor. I used to think at the factory, so they fired me. . . ."

All the workmen were silent as they looked at Voshchev. Their faces were indifferent and dull; a rare thought, tired before it started, occasionally lit their patient eyes.

"What's this truth of yours?" said the man who spoke before. "You don't work, you don't experience the substance of living. So where can you remember thought from?"

"And what do you need this truth for?" asked another man, opening his lips that had been stuck together from long silence. "You'll feel good only inside your mind, and outside it will still be rotten."

"I suppose you know everything already?" Voshchev asked with faint, timid hope.

"What d'you think? We give life to all organizations!" answered the short man with the parched mouth, around which the beard grew sparsely from exhaustion.

At this moment the door opened, and Voshchev saw last night's mower with a teakettle for the work brigade. The water had already boiled up on the stove out in the yard. The hour of waking was over; it was time to nourish the body for the day's work.

A country clock hung on the wooden wall and ticked patiently, worked by its dead weights. A pink flower was painted on its face to give cheer to everyone who looked at the time. The workmen sat down in a row along the table. The mower, who did woman's work in the barrack, sliced the bread and gave each man a piece, adding a chunk of last night's cold meat. The workmen began to chew earnestly, ingesting the food as a duty, but not enjoying it. Although they had knowledge of the meaning of life, which is equivalent to eternal happiness, their faces were gloomy and emaciated, and instead of peace they showed weariness.

Voshchev watched those sadly living men, who could hold the truth within themselves without rejoicing, with timid hope and fear of loss. It pleased him just to know that truth existed in the world inside the body of the man next to him, who had spoken to him only a moment ago. Perhaps it was enough to be near that man to become patient with life and capable of work.

"Come eat with us!" the eating men invited Voshchev.

He stood up and, still without complete faith in the general necessity of the world, went to eat, shy and troubled.

"Why are you so skimpy?" they asked him.

"Just so," he answered. "But now I also want to work on the substance of life."

All through the time that he had doubted the rightness of life, he seldom ate calmly, always feeling the torment of his spirit. But now he ate quietly, and the most active of the workmen, Comrade Safronov, told him after breakfast that maybe he would do, since people, like materials, were now hard to get. The union deputy had been combing all the towns and empty places around for days, looking for some landless poor that could be turned into permanent workers, but he seldom brought anyone. Everybody was busy living and working.

Voshchev had already eaten his fill and got up among the sitting men.

"Why are you standing up?" Safronov asked him.

"I can't think as well sitting down. I'd rather stand a while."

"All right, stand. You must be one of the intelligentsia —all they want is to hang around and think."

"When I wasn't thinking, I lived by manual labor. But afterwards, I couldn't understand the meaning of life, and so I lost my strength."

Some music approached the barrack and began to play special, lively sounds, in which there was no thought, but a triumphant premonition that made Voshchev's body quaver with joy. The troubling sounds of the sudden music aroused a feeling of conscience; they urged one to care for the time of life, to travel the whole distance toward hope and reach it, and find there the source of this exciting song, so that one wouldn't have to cry at dying time over the misery of a wasted existence.

The music stopped, and life settled back in everybody with all its former weight.

The trade union deputy, whom Voshchev had already met, entered the barrack and asked the whole brigade to walk across the old town again, so the workmen would grasp the meaning of the work they were to begin on the mowed lot after the march.

The work brigade came out and stopped, embarrassed, in front of the musicians. Safronov pretended to cough, shy at the public honor directed at him in the form of music. The excavator Chiklin stared with wonder and expectation —he did not feel especially worthy, but he longed to hear once more the solemn march and rejoice in silence. Others timidly dropped their patient hands.

The union deputy was too busy and active to remember himself, and this made things easier for him. In the bustle of welding the masses and organizing auxiliary joys and benefits for the workers, he forgot to think about satisfaction in the pleasures of personal life; he lost weight and slept heavily at night. If the union deputy had reduced the flurry of his work and recalled the shortages of household goods in his family, or stroked at night his shrunken, aging body, he would have felt ashamed of his existence at the expense of two percent of suffering labor. But he could not stop for contemplative thought.

With a haste resulting from his restless devotion to working men, the union deputy stepped forward to show the skilled workmen the town which lay scattered in separate households, because today they had to start construction of the single building where the entire local proletariat would come to live. And this common building was to rise above the whole town of individual homes and courtyards. The small one-family homes would be vacated and impermeably overgrown with vegetation, and the remaining, withered humans of forgotten times would gradually breathe their last in them.

Several bricklayers from two factories under construction came up to the barrack. The union deputy was straining with the enthusiasm of the last moments before the start of the builders' march across the town. The musicians brought the mouthpieces of the wind instruments to their lips. But the work brigade was standing here and there, unprepared to march. Safronov noticed the false diligence in the faces of the musicians and felt insulted for the music.

"What kind of game is that now? Where do we have to go—what's there we didn't see!"

The union deputy's face lost its expression of readiness and he became aware of his soul—he always felt it when he was offended.

"Comrade Safronov! The District Trade Union Bureau wanted to show your first model brigade the misery of the old life, the various shabby houses and sad conditions, as well as the cemetery where proletarians who died without happiness before the revolution used to be buried. Then you would see what a ruined city was lying here on the wide plain of our country, and you would realize at once why we must have a common building for the proletariat, which you will start constructing after the . . ."

"Don't be so damned overzealous!" Safronov told him. "Haven't we seen the shabby little houses where all sorts of authorities are living? Take your music to the children's organization; we'll manage to build the house with our own political consciousness."

"So I'm overzealous?" The union deputy got worried, guessing at his meaning. "We've got a fellow in the union bureau who'll sing hallelujah to everything, and you say I am overzealous?"

And, with a sore heart, the union deputy silently went off to the union office, the band following him.

The mowed plot smelled of dead grass and the dampness of denuded earth, which emphasized the general sadness of life and futility. Voshchev was given a spade, and he clutched at it as if he hoped to dig the truth out of the dust. In his own deprivation, Voshchev would even have consented to having no meaning of his own in existence, but he wanted at least to see it in the substance of the body of another man; and to be near that man he was ready to offer up in labor his feeble body, wearied out by thought and lack of meaning.

In the middle of the empty lot stood the engineer. He was not an old man, and he wasn't gray from the natural count of years. He regarded the whole world as dead matter and judged it by those parts of it which he had already transformed into constructions. The world yielded everywhere to his attentive and imagining mind, limited only by his awareness of the inertness of nature. Material always submitted to precision and patience; hence, it was inanimate and empty. But man was alive and worthy in the midst of dismal matter. Therefore the engineer was smiling politely at the workmen.

Voshchev saw that the engineer's cheeks were pink, but not from stoutness; they were pink from the excessive beating of his heart. And Voshchev was pleased that this man had an excited and beating heart.

The engineer told Chiklin that he had already planned out the ground work and marked the area of the foundation pit. He showed him the pegs that had been set out in the ground. They could start now. Chiklin listened to the engineer and checked his plan against his own mind and experience. During the excavation work he was the brigade leader—digging the foundation pit was his best skill. When it was time for masonry, Safronov would take over.

"Not enough hands," Chiklin said to the engineer. "It will be slow torture, not work. The time spent will eat up all benefit."

"The Labor Exchange promised to send fifty men, and

I asked for a hundred," said the engineer. "But you and I will be the ones to answer for the job. You're the leading brigade."

"We won't lead, we'll make everybody else pull up alongside. If only the men would turn up."

And Chiklin plunged his spade into the soft surface of the earth, concentrating his impassively reflective face upon the ground. Voshchev also began to dig deep into the soil, sending his whole strength into the spade. Now he admitted the possibility that children would grow up, that joy would be transformed into thought, and that future man would find peace in that solidly built house and look out of the high windows into the spreading world awaiting him outside. He had already destroyed forever thousands of grass shoots, rootlets, and little underground shelters of assiduous creatures, and was now working in a trench of dreary clay. But Chiklin was way ahead of him. He had long put down the spade and taken up a crowbar to crumble the hard, compressed rock below the clay. Chiklin was abolishing the ancient natural order without ability to understand it.

Conscious of the smallness of his brigade, Chiklin hurried as he broke up the age-old ground, turning all the energy of his body into blows at dead places. His heart beat at its customary pace, the strength of his patient back was draining out in sweat; Chiklin had no protective fat under his skin—his old veins and guts were close to the surface. He sensed his surroundings without any thought or consciousness, but with precision. Once upon a time he had been younger, and women loved him, greedy for his powerful body that wandered here and there and gave itself to all without thought of preserving itself. Many people had needed Chiklin at that time; they needed the shelter and peace of his faithful warmth. But he wanted to give shelter to too many, so as to feel enough himself; and then women and friends would leave him out of jealousy, and Chiklin, lonely in the nights, would go out into the market square and overturn the stalls, or carry them off somewhere else altogether, for which he later languished in jail, where he sang songs on cherry-red summer evenings.

By noon Voshchev's zeal turned up less and less soil, the digging began to tire and irritate him, and he fell behind the brigade. Only one skinny workman was slower than himself. This laggard was glum and puny in his whole body; the sweat of weakness dripped into the clay from his dim monotonous face, with sparse hair growing all around it. When he lifted the soil to the edge of the pit, he coughed, forcing the phlegm out of himself; then, quieting down, he would close his eyes, as if about to go to sleep.

"Kozlov," Safronov shouted to him. "You're feeling bad again?"

"Again," Kozlov answered in a child's pale voice.

"Too much pleasure," said Safronov. "Next time we'll make you sleep on the table right under the lamp, so you'll be ashamed and lie still."

Kozlov glanced at Safronov with red, moist eyes and kept silent in the indifference of fatigue.

"Why does he pick on you?" asked Voshchev.

Kozlov dug a bit of dirt out of his bony nose and looked sideways, as if longing for freedom, but not really longing for anything.

"They're saying," Kozlov forced out the words with the difficulty of an offended man, "that I have no woman, so I love myself at night under the blanket, and in the daytime I'm no good for life because my body's drained. They think they know everything!"

Voshchev returned to digging the unchanging clay and saw that there still remained a lot of clay and earth. You needed to have life for a long time to overcome with labor and forgetfulness this age-old cumulate world that hid within its darkness the truth of all existence. It might be easier to think out life's meaning inside your head; after all, you might guess it by chance or brush against it with sadly flowing feeling.

"Safronov," said Voshchev, his patience weakening. "I'd rather think without working. You can't dig down to the bottom of the whole world anyway."

"You'll never get anywhere," Safronov declared without halting. "You'll have no memory, and you'll become like Kozlov—just knowing your own self, like an animal."

"Quit moaning, orphan!" Chiklin said from up in front. "Look at other people, and live, so long as you were born."

Voshchev glanced at the men and decided to live somehow, since they also endured and lived: he came into the world with them, and he would die when his time came inseparably from them.

"Lie down on your face, Kozlov, catch your breath," said Chiklin. "He coughs, and sighs, and suffers, and keeps quiet. You dig graves that way, not houses."

But Kozlov had no use for anybody's pity. He stroked his feeble, dull breast inside his shirt when nobody could see and went on digging the tenacious ground. He still believed that life would come after the construction of big buildings and was afraid that he would not be accepted into that life if he presented himself there as a miserable element incapable of work. In the mornings, Kozlov was troubled by one feeling—his heart found it difficult to beat; nevertheless, he hoped to live in the future with at least a little remnant of his heart. Because his chest was weak, though, he had to stroke his bones from time to time at work, urging them in a whisper to endure.

Midday was gone, but the Labor Exchange had not sent any diggers. Last night's mower awakened, boiled potatoes, poured eggs over them, buttered them, added yesterday's leftover gruel, sprinkled some dill on top for luxury, and brought this mess of food in a kettle to build up the depleted strength of the brigade.

They ate silently, without looking at each other and without greed, placing no value on the food, as though a man's strength came from consciousness alone.

The engineer had made his daily rounds of various inevitable institutions and came to the foundation site. He stood aside for a while, until the men finished the food in the kettle, then he said:

"On Monday we'll have forty more men. And today is Saturday—time for you to quit."

"What do you mean quit?"asked Chiklin. "We'll get another cube or so out of the pit. No point in quitting before that."

"You have to quit now," the engineer, who directed the construction, argued. "You've been working over six hours, and there's a law about that."

"That law was made only for tired elements," Chiklin protested. "And I still have a bit of strength left before going to sleep. What do you think?" he asked the others.

"It's a long way till evening," said Safronov. "Why waste life? Better accomplish something. After all, we aren't animals, we can live for the sake of enthusiasm."

"Maybe nature will show us something down below," said Voshchev.

"What!" one of the workmen asked.

The engineer nodded; he was afraid of empty time at home and did not know how to live alone.

"In that case I'll go and do a little drafting too, and calculate the pile sockets again."

"Sure, go ahead," Chiklin approved. "The earth is dug up anyway, it's dull around here. We'll finish up, then fix the time for living, and take a rest."

The engineer slowly walked away. He recalled his childhood, when on holiday eves the servant washed the floors, his mother tidied up the rooms, unpleasant water flowed down the street, and he, a boy, did not know what to do, and felt lonely, and wondered about things. Now too the weather was turning dark, slow clouds drifted in the sky above the plain, and all over Russia people were washing floors on the eve of the holiday of socialism. Somehow it was still too early to enjoy things, and no point to it either.

Better to sit down, think, and keep drafting the parts of the future building.

Kozlov felt the pleasure of a full stomach and his mind improved.

"Masters of the whole world, as they say, and look how they love their grub," he spoke his thought. "A master would build himself a house in a wink, and you will end your lives on the bare ground."

"You're a swine, Kozlov," declared Safronov. "What do you need the proletariat in the house for if you take pleasure only from your own body?"

"And what if I do?" Kozlov replied. "Who ever loved me, even once? Endure, they keep saying, have patience till old man capitalism dies. So now it's dead, and I am living alone again under the blanket. Don't I feel sad, too?"

Voshchev was stirred with friendship toward Kozlov.

"Sadness doesn't mean a thing, Comrade Kozlov," he said. "It shows that our class feels the whole world, and happiness is a far-off business anyway. . . . Happiness will only lead to shame!"

Then Voshchev and the others got to work again. The sun was still high and the birds sang plaintively in the bright air, without elation but seeking food in space. Swallows darted low over the bowed, digging men; their wings grew silent with fatigue, and the sweat of poverty was under their down and feathers. They had been flying since sunup without ceasing to torment themselves to feed their wives and chicks. Once Voshchev picked up a bird that had died instantly in midair and dropped down to the ground. It was soaked with sweat. And when Voshchev plucked it to see its body, a pitiful, meager creature lay in his hands, dead from the exhaustion of its labor. And now Voshchev did not spare himself in breaking up the solidly fused ground; a building would be raised here, in which people would be shielded from misfortunes, and they would throw crumbs out of their windows to the birds living outside.

Chiklin bore down heavily on the crowbar, fracturing the clay without seeing the birds or the sky, without thought, and his flesh wore itself out in the clay ditch, but he wasn't troubled by his fatigue; he knew that his body would replenish itself in nightly sleep.

The weary Kozlov sat down on the ground and chipped away at the bared limestone with an axe. He worked, forgetting time and place, pouring out the remnants of his warm strength into the stone he was splitting; the stone grew warm, and Kozlov was gradually turning cold. He could have died there unnoticed, and the broken stone would have been his poor legacy to future, growing people. His trousers crept up as he moved, the bent sharp shin bones under his tight skin were like jagged knives. Those helpless, unprotected bones made Voshchev depressingly anxious; it seemed to him that the bones would tear the flimsy skin and be exposed. He touched his own legs in the same bony places and said to everyone:

"Time to take off! You'll wear yourself out and die, and who will be the people then?"

Voshchev did not hear a single word in answer. Evening was drawing near; the blue night was rising in the distance, promising sleep and a breath of coolness. The dead sky hung over the earth like sadness. Kozlov went on crushing the stone in the ground, never moving his eyes from it, and his weakened heart was probably beating without joy.

The engineer who directed the building of the all-proletarian house came out of his drafting office late in the darkness of the night. The foundation pit was empty. The work brigade was sleeping in the barrack in a close row of bodies, and only the light of the dimmed lamp seeped out through the cracks between the boards, holding out a faint glow in case of emergency or for anyone who might suddenly want a drink of water. The engineer Prushevsky walked up to the barrack and peered inside through a knot-hole. Nearest to the wall lay Chiklin; his hand, swollen with strength, rested on his stomach, and his whole body rumbled in the nourishing work of sleep. The barefoot Kozlov slept with an open mouth; there was a rattling in his throat, as though the air he breathed passed through dark, heavy blood, and now and then tears rolled out of his pale, half-open eyes—from dreams, or some unknown longing.

Prushevsky drew his head away from the boards, thinking. Far away the factory construction project glowed with electricity, but Prushevsky knew that there was nothing there except inanimate building materials and tired, un-thinking men. It had been his idea to build a single proletarian house instead of the old town, where people still lived in fenced-in yards. Within a year the whole local proletariat would leave the petty properties of the town and come to live in the monumental new building. In ten or twenty years another engineer would build a tower in the middle of the world, and the working people of the whole earth would enter it for permanent happy settle-ment. Prushevsky could already envisage the masterpiece of static mechanics—in the sense of its art and fitness—that should be set up in the center of the world. But he could not foretell the structure of the souls of the tenants of the common house he was building in the midst of that plain, nor could he even visualize the residents of the future tower in the center of the universal earth. What kind of bodies would youth have at that time, and what stirring power would make hearts beat and minds think?

Prushevsky wanted to know all this, at once, so that the walls of his construction would not rise in vain. The build-ing must be tenanted with people, and people must be full of that excess of warm life that used to be called soul. He was afraid of erecting empty buildings, in which people would live only to keep out of bad weather.

Prushevsky was chilled in the night and climbed down

into the pit the men had started digging. It was quiet there. For a while he sat in its depth; beneath him was rock; at his side was the slope of cut ground, and he could see the soil resting on the layer of clay without originating from it. Did every base give rise to a superstructure? Did every production of materials required for life generate man's soul as a by-product? And if production were to be perfected to an exact economy, would unexpected by-products come out of it as well?

Already at the age of twenty-five, the engineer Prushevsky had begun to feel the restriction of his consciousness and the limit to any further understanding of life—as though a dark wall had risen before his feeling mind. And ever since then he had been tormented, groping at his wall and trying to reassure himself that, essentially, the most central, the true structure of the substance of which the world and mankind were composed had already been grasped by him; that all the necessary science lay within the wall of his awareness, and beyond it there was only a dull, insignificant place toward which there was no need to strive. And yet, it was interesting to know: had anybody else climbed out beyond the wall? Prushevsky went back to the barrack, bent down again and looked inside at the nearest sleeper, hoping to discover in the sleeper something about life that was unknown to him. But he could see very little because the kerosene had almost burned down in the night lamp, and all that he could hear was slow, falling breath. Prushevsky left the barrack and went to get a shave in the barber shop for the night-shift. When he felt sad, he liked to feel the touch of someone's hand.

It was after midnight when Prushevsky came home to his apartment in a small outbuilding in an orchard. He opened the window into the darkness and sat down a while. A faint local breeze stirred the leaves now and then. Then silence would return. Behind the orchard someone walked and sang a song. It may have been an accountant, returning from evening work, or simply some man who was bored by sleep.

Far off, suspended and without hope of salvation, a dim star glowed, and would never come any nearer. Prushevsky looked at it through the misty air; time was passing, and he questioned himself:

"Shall I die?"

Prushevsky could not see who needed him enough to make it so necessary for him to keep himself alive until his death, which was still far away. Instead of hope, he had only patience left; and somewhere beyond the succession of nights, beyond the blossoming and the decline of gardens, beyond the people encountered and lost, there was a time when he would have to stretch out on his cot, turn his face to the wall, and die, without ever having learned to weep. Only his sister would still be living in the world, but she would give birth to a child, and pity for the child would become stronger than grief for her dead, ruined brother.

I had better die, thought Prushevsky. I am used, but no one takes any joy in me. Tomorrow I will write the last letter to my sister, I must buy a stamp in the morning.

And, having resolved to die, he lay down in bed and fell asleep with the happiness of indifference to life. Before he had time to savor his full happiness, he was awakened by it at three o'clock in the morning, and, turning on the light in his room, he sat in the brightness and silence till dawn, surrounded by the nearby apple trees. Then he opened his window to hear the birds and the steps of passersby.

After the general awakening, an outsider entered the excavators' sleeping barrack. Among the workmen, the only one who knew him was Kozlov, because of previous conflicts. He was Comrade Pashkin, chairman of the Area Trade Union Council. His face was already elderly and his body stooped—not so much from the number of his years as from the load of public responsibilities. Because of all this, he spoke in a fatherly manner, and knew or foresaw almost everything.

"Oh, well," he was in the habit of saying at difficult moments. "Happiness will come historically all the same." And he would bow submissively his dreary head, which no longer needed to think about anything.

Pashkin stood a while near the foundation pit, his face bent to the ground, as it always was to everything that was being worked on.

"Too slow," he said to the workmen. "Why do you begrudge raising productivity? Socialism will get along without you, but without it you'll live in vain and die out."

"We're trying, as they say, Comrade Pashkin," said Kozlov.

"How are you trying? Dug up a single pile!"

Shamed by Pashkin's reproach, the workmen were silent. They stood there and saw that the man was right: the earth should be dug faster and the house put up. Or else you'll die and never make it. Life might be passing now like the flow of breath, but by the building of the house it could be organized for later on—for future immovable happiness, and for childhood.

Pashkin glanced into the distance, at the plains and ravines. Somewhere out there the winds had their beginning, cold clouds started, all sorts of mosquitoes and sicknesses were breeding, kulaks were thinking their thoughts and backward village ignoramuses were sleeping. And the proletariat lived by itself in this dreary emptiness, and had to think of everything for everybody, and build with its own hands the substance of a long life. And Pashkin felt sorry for all his trade unions, and he knew within himself a kindness for the working people.

"I'll arrange some benefits for you, comrades, along the trade union lines," said Pashkin.

"Where will you take those benefits?" asked Safronov.

"We must first produce them and turn them over to you, and then you can give them to us."

Pashkin looked at Safronov with his gloomy foreseeing eyes and went off to his job inside the town. Kozlov walked after him and said, when they were some distance away:

"Comrade Pashkin, they've taken on Voshchev here, and he has no assignment from the labor exchange. You ought to take him back off, as they say."

"I see no conflict here, there is a shortage of proletariat nowadays," Pashkin gave his opinion and left Kozlov without consolation. And Kozlov immediately began to lose his proletarian faith and wanted to go back inside the town— to start writing discrediting reports and get various conflicts going for the sake of organizational achievements.

Up until midday the time went peacefully. None of the organizing or technical personnel came to the site, but the earth kept deepening nevertheless under the shovels, responding only to the diggers' strength and patience. From time to time Voshchev bent down and picked up a pebble or a lump of clotted earth and put it into his pocket for preservation. He was both gladdened and troubled by the almost eternal existence of the pebble in the clay, in the accumulated darkness: it meant, there was a reason for its being there, and so all the more reason for a man to live.

After midday Kozlov could no longer catch his breath. He tried to inhale seriously and deeply, but the air would not penetrate, as it had before, down to his belly, but acted only at the top. Kozlov sat down on the bared ground and touched his bony face with his hands.

"Upset yourself, eh?" Safronov asked him. "You ought to take up sports to strengthen yourself, but all you care for is conflicts. You're backward in your thinking."

Chiklin battered away at a slab of native rock without stop or mercy, never halting for a moment's thought or feeling. He did not know any reason for living differently

—who could tell, he might even turn into a thief or hurt the revolution.

"Kozlov is ailing again!" Chiklin said to Safronov. "He won't survive socialism—some function's lacking in him."

And Chiklin started thinking at once, because there was no outlet for his life the moment it stopped flowing into the ground. He leaned against the excavation wall with his damp back, glanced into the distance, and imagined memories—there was nothing else he could think about. In the ravine near the foundation pit grasses were growing sparsely and sand lay dead and useless. The unremitting sun recklessly squandered its body on every trifle of low-lying life; it was the sun, too, that had dug the ravine a long time ago by means of warm rains, but no proletarian use was being made of the ravine as yet. To verify his thought, Chiklin climbed down and measured the ravine with his usual step, breathing evenly as he counted. The ravine could be used for the foundation pit; it was merely necessary to calculate the slopes and dig to a waterproof depth.

"Let Kozlov be sick a while," said Chiklin when he came back. "We won't try to dig here any more—we'll sink the building into the ravine and raise it up from there: Kozlov will last till it's ready."

When they heard Chiklin, many of the workmen stopped digging and sat down for a rest. But Kozlov had already recovered from his fatigue and wanted to go to Prushevsky, to report that the digging had stopped and it was necessary to take disciplinary measures. Preparing to perform this organizational service, Kozlov rejoiced and recovered in advance. However, Sofronov stopped him the moment he moved off the spot.

"What's that, Kozlov? Aiming to get next to the intelligentsia? There it is, coming down to our masses itself."

Prushevsky was approaching the foundation pit ahead of some unknown people. He had sent off the letter to his sister and now he wanted to act persistently, worrying only about immediate things and constructing any building for anybody else's benefit, just so as not to trouble his mind, in which he had established a special delicate indifference, in accord with death and the orphaned state of the surviving people. He was especially tender with those people whom, for one reason or another, he had formerly disliked; now he sensed within them almost the main riddle of his life, and he studied attentively the alien and familiar stupid faces, agitated and unable to understand them.

The unknown people turned out to be new workmen, sent by Pashkin to assure proper government tempos. But the new arrivals were not workers. Chiklin immediately recognized them as civil employees retrained the other way around, various hermits from the steppe, and men accustomed to walk slowly in the field behind toiling horses. Their bodies gave no evidence of proletarian talent for work; they were more capable of lying on their backs or resting in some other way.

Prushevsky told Chiklin to assign the workmen to places in the foundation pit and give them training, because it was necessary to live and work with whatever people existed on earth.

"We don't mind," Safronov said. "We'll knock their backwardness straight out into activity."

"That's it," said Prushevsky, trusting him, and followed Chiklin down into the ravine.

Chiklin said that the ravine was more than half of the foundation pit, ready-made, and that by using it weak men could be preserved for the future. Prushevsky agreed, since he was going to die before the building was finished anyway.

"And I feel the stirring of scientific doubt," Safronov objected, wrinkling his politely class-conscious face. And everybody listened to him, while Safronov looked at them with a smile of mysterious intelligence.

"Where did Comrade Chiklin get his idea of the world?" Safronov uttered slowly. "Or did he receive some special kiss in infancy so he can choose the ravine better than an educated man? How come you're doing all the thinking, Comrade Chiklin, and I and Comrade Prushevsky go around like nobodies among the classes, without seeing any way to betterment?"

Chiklin was too sullen for cunning and answered approximately:

"There's no place for life to go, so you think in your head."

Prushevsky glanced at Chiklin as at a purposeless martyr, then ordered a test drilling in the ravine and returned to his office. There he went to work diligently on the parts of the proletarian house he had planned, so as to feel things and forget people. About two hours later Voshchev brought him samples of ground from the drill holes. He must know the meaning of natural life, Voshchev thought silently about Prushevsky, and, tormented by his persistent misery, he asked:

"Do you happen to know the reason why the whole world was constructed?"

Prushevsky halted his attention on Voshchev: Will THEY be an intelligentsia too? Can it be that WE are twins begot by capitalism? Good God, what a dreary face he has already!

"I don't know," he answered.

"You should have learned it, if they tried to teach you."

"Each one of us was taught some dead part: I know clay, the weight of gravity, and static mechanics, but I have little knowledge of machines, and I don't know why the heart beats in an animal. They didn't explain to us things as a whole, or what's inside."

"Too bad," Voshchev declared. "Then how could you live so long? Clay is all right for bricks—it's not enough for us!"

Prushevsky took up a sample of the ravine soil and concentrated on it. He longed to remain alone with that dark lump of earth. Voshchev retreated behind the door and disappeared, whispering his own sorrow to himself.

The engineer examined the bit of ground and then, by the inertia of independently functioning reason, free of hope and desire for fulfillment, he calculated for a long time how compression and deformation would affect that ground. Formerly, when he was alive in his senses and saw happiness, Prushevsky would have done his calculations with less precision. But now he wanted to apply himself continuously to objects and constructions, to fill his mind and empty heart with them, in place of friendship and affection for people. Concentration on the static technology of the future building provided Prushevsky with the indifference of a clear mind that was almost like pleasure; and the details aroused in him a stronger and firmer interest than comradely excitement with others who shared his views. Eternal matter, requiring neither motion, nor life, nor extinction, replaced for Prushevsky something forgotten and essential, such as the being of a lost beloved.

When he completed his calculations, Prushevsky made sure of the immutability of the future all-proletarian building and felt consoled by the strength of the material destined to shelter people who had lived outdoors until then. And he was filled with a lightness and quiet, as though he were not existing indifferently before death, but living the life about which his mother had once whispered to him with her lips—he had lost it even in memory.

Without disturbing his feeling of peace and wonder, Prushevsky left the earthworks office. Outside, the emptied summer day was drawing into evening; everything near and far was gradually ending; birds hid themselves, people lay down to sleep, smoke curled peacefully over distant huts in the field, where unknown tired people sat by the kettle, waiting for supper, having decided to endure life to the end. The foundation pit was empty; the diggers had gone to work in the ravine, and all movement was there now. Prushevsky had a sudden desire to be in the big city far away, where people slept long, thought and argued, where food stores were open in the evenings, smelling of wine and pastries, where you might meet an unknown woman and talk with her all night, feeling the mysterious happiness of friendship that makes you want to live forever in such disquiet; and then, after saying good-bye under the already extinguished gas lamp, you'd separate in the empty dawn without promise of further meetings.

Prushevsky sat down on the bench near the office. He used to sit like that outside his father's house—summer evenings had not changed since then—and watch the people passing by. Some of them he liked, and he regretted that everybody did not know everybody else. And one feeling was still alive within him and troubled him to this day. Once, on such an evening, a girl passed by the house where he had spent his childhood. He could neither recall her face, nor the year when it happened, but ever since he had been looking into every woman's face, and never recognized the one who, having vanished, was nonetheless the only one for him. And she had passed so near, without stopping.

During the revolution, dogs barked day and night throughout Russia, but now they were silent: the time of work had come, and the laborers slept in peace. The militia guarded the quiet of workers' dwellings from without, to make sure sleep was deep and nourishing for the morning's toil. Only the night-shift builders did not sleep, and the legless invalid whom Voshchev met on coming to that city. Today he rolled in his low cart to Comrade Pashkin, to get from him his share of life, for which he came every week.

Pashkin lived in a solid brick house, so he wouldn't be burned to death, and the open windows of his dwelling looked out on the park of culture, where flowers glowed in the light even at nighttime. The cripple rolled past the kitchen which hummed like a boiler room, producing supper, and stopped in front of Pashkin's office. The master of the house sat at his desk without motion, deep in thought about something invisible to the invalid. On the desk stood various liquids and jars for strengthening health and developing activity. Pashkin had acquired for himself a lot of class consciousness; he was in the vanguard; he had already accumulated enough achievements, and therefore he took care of his body scientifically—not only for the personal joy of existence, but also for the sake of the working masses close to him. The invalid waited while Pashkin, getting up from his occupation of thinking, ran through a quick set of exercises with all his limbs and, restoring freshness, sat down again. The cripple wanted to say what he had come to say through the window, but Pashkin picked up a little medicine bottle, sighed slowly three times, and drank a drop.

"How long am I going to wait for you?" asked the invalid, who was not conscious of the value of either life or health. "You want to get it from me again?"

Pashkin unwittingly became agitated, but calmed himself with an effort of mind—he never wanted to waste the nerves of his body.

"What's the matter, Comrade Zhachev? What is it you lack? Why all the excitement?"

Zhachev answered directly according to fact:

"You bourgeois, have you forgotten why I'm putting up with you? D'you want a load in your appendix? Just remember—no law is strong enough for me!"

The invalid pulled out a clump of roses close at hand and flung them away without making any use of them.

"Comrade Zhachev," answered Pashkin. "I can't understand you at all—you're getting the top pension, first category—so what's it all about? I've always met you halfway in every way I could."

"You're lying, you class leftover—it wasn't you who met me, it's me who's always gotten in your way!"

Pashkin's wife, with red lips, chewing meat, came into the office.

"Again you're upsetting yourself, Levochka," she said.

"I'll bring a package for him in a minute. It's become simply unbearable, the strongest nerves will wear out with these people!"

She went out, her whole impossible body in a dither.

"Look at the wife he's fattened up, the scum!" said Zhachev from the garden. "Idling with all her valves. So you can manage such a b . . . !"

Pashkin was too experienced in leading backward elements to get upset.

"You could also get yourself a life's companion, Comrade Zhachev: your pension provides for all the minimal needs."

"Oh–o, the tactful vermin!" Zhachev declared from the dark. "My pension won't even buy me gruel. And I want fats, and some dairy. Tell your slut to pour me a bottle of cream—but good and thick!"

Pashkin's wife came into her husband's room with a bundle.

"Olya, he's demanding cream now," said Pashkin.

"What else! Maybe we ought to buy him crepe de chine for his pants? The things you'll think of!"

"She wants me to slit her skirt in the street," said Zhachev from the flowerbed. "Or smash her bedroom window —right to the powder table where she plasters her snout. I see she wants to get a little present from me!"

Pashkin's wife remembered how Zhachev had sent a letter of denunciation against her husband to the Regional Party Committee, and the investigation lasted a whole month. They had even picked on his name: why Lev, and why Ilyich* on top of it? It should be one or the other! And so she immediately brought the invalid a bottle of cooperative cream, and Zhachev, receiving the parcel and the bottle through the window, made his departure from the garden.

"I'll check the quality of the products at home," he said, halting his conveyance at the gate. "If there's again a piece

*Translator's Note: Satirical allusion to *Lev* Trotsky and Vladimir *Ilyich* Lenin.

of spoiled meat or some leftovers, expect a brick in the belly: according to humanity I'm better than you—I need appropriate food."

Left alone with his spouse, Pashkin could not get rid of his anxiety over the cripple till midnight. Pashkin's wife knew how to think up ways out of trouble, and this is what she thought up during the family silence:

"You know what, Levochka? Why not organize Zhachev somehow, and then move him up to some post—say, leading the maimed! After all, every man needs to have at least a little sense of power, then he is quiet and decent. . . . I must say, Levochka, you're altogether too trusting and absurd!"

When Pashkin heard his wife, he was filled with love and quiet—his basic life returned to him again.

"Olgusha, my little frog, but you have a colossal sense of the masses! Let me organize myself next to you just for that!"

He laid his head upon his wife's body and kept still in the enjoyment of happiness and warmth. Night continued in the garden, Zhachev's cart was creaking in the distance; this creaking was a sign to all the little people of the town that there was no butter, for Zhachev greased his cart only with butter, which he received in the bundles of the wealthier residents. He deliberately wasted the product to keep the bourgeois bodies from gaining additional strength, but he himself refused to consume this prosperous substance. During the past two days Zhachev had for some reason felt the urge to see Nikita Chiklin, and he directed the movement of his cart toward the foundation pit.

"Nikit!" he called at the sleeping barrack. After the sound the night, the silence, and the general sadness of feeble life in the dark became still deeper. No answer came from the barrack; Zhachev heard only feeble breathing.

Without sleep the workingman would have died long ago, thought Zhachev—and he rolled away without noise.

But two men came out of the ravine with a lantern, so they could see Zhachev.

"Who are you? Why so short?" Safronov's voice asked.

"It's me," said Zhachev, "because capital cut me down in half. Is one of you two Nikita by any chance?"

"It's not an animal, but a man all right!" the same Safronov answered. "Tell him what you're thinking, Chiklin."

With his lantern Chiklin lit up Zhachev's face and his short body, then turned the lantern away toward the darkness in embarrassment.

"What's the matter, Zhachev?" Chiklin said quietly. "You've come for some porridge? Come along, we have enough left over, it'll sour by tomorrow, we'll have to throw it out anyway."

Chiklin was afraid that Zhachev would be offended by the offer of help and wanted him to eat the porridge with the feeling that it wasn't anybody's any more and would be thrown out anyway. Zhachev used to visit him before as well, when Chiklin worked at clearing the river of fallen trees and branches, to get his nourishment from the working class. But in midsummer he changed his course and began to eat at the expense of the maximum class, by which he hoped to be of use to the whole unpropertied movement toward future happiness.

"I've missed you," said Zhachev. "I'm tortured by the presence of scum, and I want to ask you when you'll finish building your rubbish here, so the city can be burned down!"

"Try and grow wheat on a burdock!" said Safronov about the cripple. "We squeeze our bodies dry for the general building, and he brings up a slogan that our condition is rubbish—and not a moment of conscious sense anywhere!"

Safronov knew that socialism was a scientific business, and his words were also logical and scientific, equipped for strength with two meanings—one basic and one extra, for reserve like any other material. The three men had already reached the barrack and entered. Voshchev took from the corner a kettle of porridge, wrapped in a quilted jacket to keep it warm, and gave it to the new arrivals. Chiklin and Safronov were badly chilled and covered with clay and dampness; they had gone to the foundation pit to dig down to the underground spring and lock it for good with solid clay.

Zhachev did not unwrap his bundle but ate the common porridge, both to satisfy his hunger and to confirm his equality with the two other men who ate. After the meal, Chiklin and Safronov went out—for a breath of air and a look around before going to sleep. And so they stood there for a time. The dark starry night was not in keeping with the toilsome earth of the ravine and the dense, discordant breathing of the sleeping diggers. If one looked only along the ground at the dry insignificant soil and the grasses existing in crowded poverty, there was no hope in life; the general universal paltriness, as well as ignorant human gloom, puzzled Safronov and undermined his ideological position. He'd even begun to doubt the happy future, which he imagined as a blue summer lit by a motionless sun: everything around him was too dim and futile both by day and by night.

"Why do you live so silently, Chiklin? Why don't you say or do something that would give me some joy?"

"What am I to do—throw my arms around you, or what?" Chiklin answered. "We'll dig the foundation pit, and that'll be fine. . . . But those fellows sent here by the Labor Exchange—why don't you give them a talking to? They keep sparing their bodies at work, as though they have something precious in them!"

"That I can," Safronov answered. "I sure can! I'll turn all those shepherds and scribblers into the working class before you count three. I'll get them digging so hard, their whole mortal element will come out in their face. . . . But why does the field lie there so sadly, Nikit? Is there misery inside the whole world, and we're the only ones with the five-year plan inside us?"

Chiklin had a small stony head, thickly covered with hair, because all his life he had either swung a hammer, or dug with a spade, and never had time to think; and so he didn't clear away Safronov's doubts.

They sighed in the fallen silence and went to bed. Zhachev was already bent over in his cart, sleeping as best he could, and Voshchev lay flat on his back and looked up with the patience of curiosity.

"You said you knew everything in the world," said Voshchev, "but all you do is dig the earth and sleep! I'd better leave you all, and go begging at the collective farms. I'm ashamed to live without the truth anyway."

Safronov assumed a definite expression of superiority on his face, and passed by the legs of the sleepers with the light tread of leadership.

"Eh-h, tell me, comrade, if you please, in what shape do you wish to get this product—round or liquid?"

"Leave him alone," said Chiklin. "We all live in an empty world; do *you* have peace of mind?"

Safronov, who loved the beauty of life and civility of mind, stood in respect of Voshchev's destiny, though at the same time he was deeply agitated: wasn't truth merely a class enemy? For, after all, the enemy could now present himself even in the form of a dream or imagination!

"Wait with your declaration for a while, Comrade Chiklin," Safronov addressed him with full significance. "The question has risen as a matter of principle, and it must be laid back according to the whole theory of feelings and mass psychosis. . . ."

"Stop cutting my wages, so to speak, Safronov," said Kozlov, awakening. "Stop making speeches when I'm asleep, or I will lodge a complaint against you! Never mind —sleep is also a kind of wage, they'll tell you all about it."

Safronov uttered a certain didactic sound, and said in his most persuasive voice: "Sleep normally, if you please, citizen Kozlov. What sort of a class of nervous intelligentsia do we have around here if a sound immediately turns into bureaucracy? And if you possess any mental stuffing, Kozlov, and lie in the vanguard, rise up on your elbow and tell us: why is it that the bourgeoisie didn't leave Comrade Voshchev any record of the universal dead inventory, and he lives at a loss and in such ridiculousness?"

But Kozlov was already asleep and felt only the depth of his body. And Voshchev turned face down and began to complain in a whisper to his own self about the mysterious life into which he had been mercilessly born.

The last of those who were still awake lay down and rested; the night was dying into dawn—and only some little animal cried somewhere at the brightening warm horizon, lamenting or rejoicing.

Chiklin sat among the sleepers and lived his life in silence; he liked at times to sit quietly and observe all he could see. Thinking was hard for him, and he sorrowed over it greatly; all he could do was feel and distress himself wordlessly. And the longer he sat, the more sadness gathered within him from lack of motion, so that he stood up and leaned with his hands against the barrack wall, just so as to press something and move into something. He had no desire at all to sleep. On the contrary, he would be glad to go into the field just now and dance with different girls under the branches, as he used to in the old times when he worked at the tile factory. The daughter of the owner had once given him a fleeting kiss; he was going down the stairs to the clay-mixing shop one June day, and she was coming up, and, raising herself on her toes, hidden under her dress, she threw her arms around his shoulders and pressed her plump, silent lips to the stubble on his cheek. Chiklin no longer remembered her face or character, but then he disliked her, as though she were some shameful creature—and so he walked past her at that time without stopping. And she, a noble creature, may have cried afterwards.

Putting on his typhus-yellow quilted jacket, his only one

since the conquest of the bourgeoisie, he muffled himself up against the night as against winter, prepared to take a walk along the road, and then, after a while, to go to sleep in the morning dew.

A man he did not recognize at first came into the sleeping barrack and stopped in the dark entranceway.

"Not sleeping yet, Comrade Chiklin!" said Prushevsky. "I'm also walking around and can't get to sleep: I keep feeling I've lost someone I can never find. . . ."

Chiklin, who respected the engineer's mind, did not know how to answer him with sympathy and was awkwardly silent.

Prushevsky sat down on a bench and bowed his head; having made up his mind to disappear from the world, he no longer felt shy with people and came to them himself.

"Forgive me, Comrade Chiklin, but I feel anxious all the time alone in my room. May I sit here till morning?"

"Why not?" said Chiklin. "Among us you'll rest quiet. Lie down in my place, and I'll find a spot for myself somewhere."

"No, I'd rather just sit. I felt sad and frightened at home, I don't know what to do. But please don't think anything wrong about me."

It hadn't even occurred to Chiklin to think anything.

"Don't go anywhere from here," he said. "We won't let anybody hurt you, don't be afraid any more."

Prushevsky sat on in the same mood; the lamp lit up his serious face, a stranger to any happy feeling. But he no longer regretted that he had acted unconsciously in coming there; in any case, he didn't have to endure much longer now, until his death and the liquidation of everything.

The sounds of conversation made Safronov open one eye a little; he wondered what was the most beneficial line to adopt toward the sleeping representative of the intelligentsia. Coming to a decision, he said:

"As far as I am informed, Comrade Prushevsky, you've sweated plenty thinking up the general proletarian living space, according to all the requisite conditions. And now, I observe, you've come at night to the proletarian masses as if some raging thing was after you! But since we have a clear line concerning specialists, lie down across from me, so you can see my face all the time and sleep without fear. . . ."

Zhachev also awakened on his cart.

"Maybe he wants to eat?" he asked about Prushevsky. "I've got some bourgeois food."

"What kind of bourgeois food, and how much nourishment does it have, Comrade?" Safronov asked with astonishment. "Where did you find bourgeois personnel?"

"Shut up, you ignorant louse!" answered Zhachev. "Your job is to come out whole in this life, and mine's to perish, to clear a space!"

"Don't be afraid," said Chiklin to Prushevsky. "Lie down and close your eyes. I'll be nearby—if you get scared, just call me."

Prushevsky, bending over to make no noise, went to Chiklin's place and lay down in his clothes.

Chiklin took off his quilted jacket and put it over his feet.

"I haven't paid my union dues for four months," Prushevsky said quietly, and, instantly feeling the cold beneath him, he covered himself. "I kept thinking there was time enough."

"Now you're mechanically out: that's a fact," Safronov declared from his place.

"Sleep silently!" said Chiklin, and went outside, to live alone a while in the sad night.

In the morning Kozlov stood for a long time over Prushevsky's sleeping body; it tormented him that this leading, intelligent person slept like an insignificant citizen among the prone masses and would now lose his authority. Kozlov had to think deeply over this puzzling circumstance. He did not want to, and he could not, permit the harm to the entire state that would result from the director's inappropriate line; he was so worried that he washed himself in a hurry, just to be prepared. At such moments in life, moments of threatening danger, Kozlov felt within himself a fiery social joy, and longed to turn this joy to some great deed and die enthusiastically, so that his whole class would hear about him and mourn him. He even shivered with ecstasy, forgetting it was summertime. He consciously went over to Prushevsky and wakened him from sleep.

"Go to your apartment, Comrade Director," he said calmly. "Our workers have not yet reached full understanding, and it won't look nice for you to go on serving in your position."

"None of your concern," said Prushevsky.

"No, if you pardon me," Kozlov objected. "Every citizen must, so to speak, carry out his directive, and you are bringing yours down and equating yourself to backward ignorants. This won't do at all. I'll go to the authorities, you're wrecking our line, you're against tempos and leadership— what kind of business is that!"

Zhachev ground his gums and kept silent, preferring to punch Kozlov in the belly that very day, but later on, as a scoundrel trying to push himself ahead. And Voshchev, hearing these words and exclamations, lay soundless, still without any understanding of life. I should have been born a mosquito: its destiny is short, he thought.

Saying nothing to Kozlov, Prushevsky rose from his place, glanced at Voshchev's familiar face, and then concentrated his look on the sleeping people. He wanted to utter the word or the request that tormented him, but a sense of sadness, like fatigue, passed over his face, and he began to walk away. Chiklin, who came from the direction of the dawn, said to Prushevsky: if he was frightened again at night, let him come again to sleep over; and if there was anything he wanted, he'd best say it.

But Prushevsky did not answer, and they silently went on their way together. The long day was starting, gloomy and hot; the sun, like blindness, hung indifferently over the low pallor of the earth; but there was no other place to live in.

"Once, long ago, when I was hardly more than a child," said Prushevsky, "I noticed, Comrade Chiklin, a girl who passed by—as young as I was then. It must have been in June or July, and since then I've been filled with longing, and began to remember and understand everything. But I never saw her after that, and I want to see her again. And there is nothing else I want any more."

"Where was it that you saw her?" asked Chiklin.

"In this same town."

"Then she must have been the daughter of a tile maker?" Chiklin guessed.

"Why?" asked Prushevsky. "I don't understand!"

"I also met her in June—and I refused to look at her then. And later, after a while, something warm came into my heart toward her, just as with you. We both saw the same person."

Prushevsky smiled modestly.

"But why?"

"Because I'll bring her to you, and you will see her—if only she's alive in the world today."

Chiklin imagined exactly Prushevsky's sorrow because he had once, though more forgetfully, suffered the same grief—over a thin, alien, light person who had silently kissed him on the left side of his face. So it was the same rare, lovely object that affected both of them from near and far.

"I'll bet she's gotten middle-aged by now," Chiklin said after a while. "She must be all worn out with troubles, and her skin has turned gray or rough like a cook's."

"Probably," Prushevsky agreed. "A lot of time has passed, and if she's still alive, she's all charred."

They halted at the edge of the ravine; they should have started much earlier to dig such an enormous pit for a general house; then the being Prushevsky needed would have existed there unharmed.

"But the likeliest thing is that she is now a conscious citizen," said Chiklin, "and works for our good: those who've had incalculable feeling in their youth get brainy afterwards."

Prushevsky looked over the empty space of the proximate landscape and felt sad that the lost companion of his life and many other needed people must live and get lost on this mortal earth where a comfortable existence had not yet been arranged, and he confided to Chiklin a grievous thought:

"But I don't know her face! How will it be, then, Comrade Chiklin, when she comes?"

Chiklin replied to him:

"You'll feel her, and recognize her—there are plenty of forgotten ones in the world! You will remember her just by your sadness."

Prushevsky understood that it was true and, afraid of somehow displeasing Chiklin, he took out his watch, to demonstrate his concern about the approaching daily toil.

Safronov, walking like an intellectual and making a pensive face, approached Chiklin.

"I've heard, Comrades, how you've been throwing your tendencies around here, and I'll ask you to be a bit more passive—it will soon be production time! And you, Comrade Chiklin, ought to keep an eye on Kozlov—he's setting his course on sabotage."

Kozlov, meantime, was eating breakfast in a gloomy mood: he considered his revolutionary services insufficient, and his daily social usefulness too small. That morning he had awakened after midnight and was tormented till morning by the fact that the main organizational construction was proceeding without his participation, and he was active only in the ravine, and not in the gigantic scale of leadership. By morning Kozlov had decided to switch to an invalid's pension and devote himself to the greatest social good—that's how painfully his proletarian conscience asserted itself.

Safronov heard of this idea from Kozlov; he classified him as a parasite and said:

"You've gotten hold of a principle for yourself, Kozlov, and you are leaving the working masses and crawling ahead. That means you're an alien louse, which always aims its course outside."

"You'd better shut up, so to speak!" answered Kozlov. "Or you'll be called to account quick enough! . . . Remember how you put up a certain poor man to slaughtering his rooster and eating him, right in the middle of collectivization? Remember? We know you tried to undercut the collectivization. We know how clear you are in your line!"

Safronov, in whom the idea was encircled by the passions of living, left Kozlov's whole argument without answer and walked away from him in his free-thinking stride. He didn't fancy having denunciations written against him.

Chiklin went up to Kozlov and asked what it was all about.

"I'm going to the social insurance today, to come out on pension," said Kozlov. "I want to keep an eye on everything, against social harm and petty-bourgeois rebellion."

"The working class isn't a Tsar," said Chiklin. "It's not afraid of rebellions."

"It may not be afraid," agreed Kozlov. "Still, as they say, it will be better to watch over it."

Zhachev was nearby in his cart. Rolling back a bit, he thrust himself forward and rammed his silent head at full speed into Kozlov's belly. Kozlov fell back from fright, losing for a moment his desire for the greatest social good. Chiklin bent down, lifted Zhachev with his carriage into the air and flung him away into space. Balancing himself in motion, Zhachev managed to say as he flew: "What for, Nikit? I wanted to make sure he gets a first-grade pension!" And then his cart was smashed, thanks to the fall, between his body and the earth.

47

"Go ahead, Kozlov!" said Chiklin to the man on the ground. "I guess we'll all take turns going there. It's time for you to get a rest."

When he came to, Kozlov declared that he'd been seeing Comrade Romanov, the chief of the Central Administration of Social Insurance, and all sorts of neatly dressed society, in his dreams, and was upset about it all week.

Soon after that Kozlov put on his jacket, and Chiklin, together with others, brushed off the earth and bits of rubbish from his clothes. Safronov had lugged Zhachev inside and, dropping his exhausted body in the corner of the barrack, he said:

"Let this proletarian substance lie here a while—some principle will grow out of it."

Kozlov shook everybody's hand and went out to retire on pension.

"Good-bye," Safronov said to him. "Now you're a sort of advance angel of the laboring personnel, seeing as you're rising to official institutions. . . ."

Kozlov could think thoughts himself; therefore he silently withdrew to a higher generally useful life, the little trunk with his belongings in his hand.

At that same moment a man who still could not be seen or stopped was running across the field beyond the ravine. His body was emaciated inside his clothes, and his pants flapped on him as if they were empty. The man reached the people and sat down by himself on a pile of earth, as a stranger to everyone. He shut one eye, and with the other he looked at the men, expecting the worst, but not about to complain; his eye was yellow like a farmer's field, and it appraised all that was visible with economic sorrow.

Soon the man heaved a sigh and lay down to doze on his belly. Nobody objected to him; there were still plenty of other people living without taking part in the construction. Besides, it was time to go to work in the ravine.

All sorts of dreams come to a laboring man at night: some express his hope fulfilled, others bring premonitions of his own coffin in a clay grave. But daytime is lived in the same stooped manner by everyone—in the patience of the body digging the earth so that the everlasting, stony root of the indestructible edifice could be set into the fresh deep pit.

The new diggers gradually settled down and got accustomed to the work. But each one devised for himself some scheme for his future escape: one hoped to accumulate experience and go to school; another waited for the moment when he could change his occupation; a third preferred to join the party and disappear in the directing apparatus. And each one diligently dug the earth, constantly remembering his idea of escape.

Pashkin visited the foundation site every second day and still complained of slow tempos. As a rule, he came on horseback, since he had sold the carriage at the time of the economy regime, and he observed the great excavation from the animal's back. However, Zhachev was always around, and he managed, whenever Pashkin went down on foot into the depths of the foundation pit, to overwater the horse, so that Pashkin now began to avoid coming on horseback but used a car instead.

Voshchev still had no feeling of the truth of life, but he reconciled himself out of the weariness of struggling with the heavy ground, and merely used his days off to collect all sorts of miserable bits of nature, as documents proving the planless creation of the world and the melancholy of every living breath.

In the evenings, which now became darker and longer, life in the barrack became dull. The peasant with the yellow eyes, who had come running from somewhere out in the fields, also lived among the work brigade; he lived silently, but redeemed his existence by doing woman's general household work, down to careful mending of frayed clothes. Safronov already wondered to himself whether it wasn't time to bring this peasant into the union as service personnel, but he didn't know how much livestock he owned in his village home, and whether he had any hired farmhands, and so he delayed his intention.

In the evenings, Voshchev lay with open eyes and longed for the future, when everything would be generally known and set in the spare feeling of happiness. Zhachev tried to convince Voshchev that his desire was insane, because the propertied enemy force was arising again and shutting out the light of life; the main thing was to cherish and protect the children, as the tenderness of the revolution, and leave them the right behest.

"What do you say, Comrades," Safronov suggested one evening, "how about installing a radio to listen to achievements and directives? We have very backward masses here who'd benefit from cultural revolution and all sorts of musical sounds, so that they won't accumulate ignorant dark moods inside themselves."

"You'd better bring an orphan girl by the hand instead of your radio," objected Zhachev.

"And what, Comrade Zhachev, might be the merits or the instructive value of your girl? What does she sacrifice for the general construction?"

"She eats no sugar now for the sake of your construction, that's how she serves it, may your unanimous soul come out of your body!" answered Zhachev.

"Ah," Safronov decided. "In that case, Comrade Zhachev, deliver us this piteous girl on your transport, and her melodious sight will make us live in greater harmony."

And Safronov stood up before everybody in the pose of a leader of enlightenment and liquidation of illiteracy. Then he paced back and forth with a convinced walk and assumed an actively thinking expression.

"Comrades, we must have here, in the form of childhood, a leader of the future proletarian world: in this matter Comrade Zhachev justified the principle that his head is whole, even if he has no legs."

Zhachev wanted to answer Safronov, but he chose instead to pull over by the pants the village peasant who stood near him, and poke him in the side twice with his well-developed fist, as a guilty bourgeois who happened to be thereabouts. The peasant's yellow eyes merely shut with pain, but he made no move to defend himself and stood silently on the ground.

"Look at 'im, the piece of iron inventory—stands there and isn't afraid," Zhachev blew up in anger and hit the peasant again with his long arm. "That means the viper had it even worse somewhere else, and with us it's paradise. Know who's in power now, you cow's husband!"

The peasant sat down to catch his breath. He was already used to getting blows from Zhachev for owning property in the village, and he soundlessly tried to overcome the pain.

"Comrade Voshchev's another who ought to acquire a punishing blow from Zhachev," said Safronov. "He's the only one among the proletariat who doesn't know what to live for."

"And what for, Comrade Safronov?" said Voshchev, who heard him from the end of the barrack. "I want the truth for the sake of productive labor."

Safronov made a gesture of moral admonition with his hand, and his face wrinkled up with the idea of pity for a backward man.

"The proletariat lives for the enthusiasm of work, Comrade Voshchev! It's time you got this tendency. Every union member's body should be aflame from this slogan!"

Chiklin was away. He was walking in the neighborhood around the tile factory. Everything looked the same as before, but now it had the shabbiness of a dying world. The trees in the street were dried out with age and had long stood leafless, but there were still some people who existed, hiding behind the double windows of the tiny houses, living more durably than the trees. In Chiklin's younger days there was the smell of a bakery here, coal-deliverers rode through the street, and loud propaganda of milk was heard from village carts. At that time, the sun of childhood warmed the dust of the roads, and his own life was an eternity amid the blue, unknown earth which Chiklin was just beginning to touch with his bare feet. But now the air of decrepitude and farewell memories hung over the extinguished bakery and the aged apple orchards.

Chiklin's constantly active sense of life led him to sadness, especially when he saw a fence by which he had sat and rejoiced in childhood: now that fence was moss-grown, bent, and old nails stuck out of it, released from the grip of the wood by the force of time. It was sad and mysterious that Chiklin had matured, forgetfully wasting his feelings, wandering in distant places and laboring variously, while the old fence stood motionless, and, remembering him, had nevertheless lasted to see the hour when Chiklin passed by it and stroked the boards, abandoned by everyone, with a hand that had forgotten happiness.

The tile factory stood in a grassy lane which no one ever walked through from one end and out of the other, because it led up to the blank wall of the cemetery. The factory building was lower now, for it was gradually sinking into the ground, and its yard was deserted. But some unknown old man was still there—sitting under the shed for raw materials and mending a pair of bast shoes, evidently meaning to return in them to the old times.

"So what do you have here now?" Chiklin asked him.

"What we have, good man, is conservation. The Soviet government is strong, and the machines here are feeble—they don't satisfy. But I hardly care anymore—I won't be breathing much longer."

Chiklin said to him:

"Of all the world's things, you've gotten only a pair of bast shoes! Wait for me here on this spot, I'll bring you some food and clothing."

"And who might you be?" asked the old man, gathering his respectful face into an attentive expression. "Are you a swindler of some sort, or just a boss—a bourgeois?"

"M-m, I'm from the proletariat," Chiklin answered reluctantly.

"Ah, so you're the present Tsar: in that case, I'll wait for you."

With a strong sense of shame and sorrow, Chiklin entered the old factory building. Soon he found the wooden stairs where the owner's daughter had once kissed him—the stairs had grown so ramshackle that they collapsed from Chiklin's weight into some nether darkness, and he could only touch their weary dust as a last farewell. After standing a while in the darkness, Chiklin discerned in it a motionless, scarcely living light, and a door leading somewhere. Behind the door was a windowless room, either forgotten or never noted in the ground plan, and a kerosene lamp was burning on the floor.

Chiklin did not know what creature had concealed itself for safety in this unknown refuge, and he stopped in the middle of the room.

Near the lamp a woman lay on the ground; the straw had already crumbled away under her body, and the woman was hardly covered by clothing. Her eyes were deeply shut, as though she were suffering or asleep, and the little girl sitting at her head was also dozing, but kept moistening her mother's lips with a piece of lemon peel, never neglecting her task. When the child came awake, she saw that her mother had grown quiet, for her lower jaw had dropped with weakness, and her dark, toothless mouth gaped open. The girl was frightened of her mother and, to allay her fear, tied the woman's mouth with a cord over the crown of her head, so that her lips were closed again. Then the girl put her face against her mother's, wanting to feel her and to go to sleep. But the mother woke lightly and said:

"Why do you sleep? Wet my lips with the lemon, you see how badly I feel."

The girl began to stroke her mother's lips again with the lemon peel. The woman lay still for a time, nourishing herself with the remnants of lemon.

"You won't fall asleep, and you won't leave me?" she asked her daughter.

"No, I'm not sleepy any more. I'll only close my eyes, but I'll think about you all the time—I will, you are my mama!"

The mother opened her eyes. They were suspicious, ready for any calamity in life, grown pale by now with indifference. She said, defending herself:

"I'm not sorry for you any more, and I don't need anybody. I've become like stone. Put out the light, and turn me on the side, I want to die."

The girl kept deliberately silent, continuing to moisten her mother's lips with the lemon peel.

"Put out the light," said the old woman. "Otherwise I see you all the time and stay alive. But don't go anywhere, you'll go after I die."

The girl blew out the lamp. Chiklin sat down on the ground, afraid to make a noise.

"Mama, are you still alive, or are you gone?" the girl asked in the dark.

"Just a little alive," the mother answered. "When you leave me, don't tell anybody that I am lying here, dead. Don't tell anybody you were born from me, or people will turn against you. Go somewhere far, far away and forget yourself there, then you will live. . . ."

"Why are you dying, mama—because you're a bourgeois, or from death?"

"Life got too sad, I'm worn out," said the mother.

"Because you were born long, long ago, and I wasn't," said the girl. "After you die, I'll never tell anybody, and nobody will know if you ever were or weren't. Only I'll go on living and remembering you in my head. You know what," she said and paused a little. "I'll fall asleep now for a little bit, even half a little bit, and you lie and think, so you won't die."

"Take the cord off me first," said the mother. "It will choke me."

But the girl was already silently asleep, and now it was altogether quiet. Chiklin could not even hear them breathing. Evidently, no creature lived in this place—no rat, no worm, nothing—there was not a sound. Only once there was a strange distant noise—perhaps an old brick fell in the next forgotten room, or the ground could no longer endure eternity and crumbled into the dust of destruction.

"Come over to me, somebody!"

Chiklin listened to the air, and cautiously began to crawl in the darkness, trying not to crush the girl as he moved. It took him a long time, because he was impeded by some trash on the way. His hand felt the girl's head, then touched the mother's face, and Chiklin bent down to her mouth, in order to find out whether it was she who had once kissed him in this house. He kissed her and recognized her by the dry taste of her lips and the slight remnant of tenderness in their fevered cracks.

"What do I need this for?" the woman said distinctly. "Now I will be forever alone." And, turning, she died with her face down.

"I must light the lamp," Chiklin said aloud, and, after some fumbling in the dark, he lit up the room.

The girl slept, her head resting on her mother's body. She curled up against the chilly underground air and warmed herself in the cramped closeness of her limbs. Chiklin wanted the child to rest and began to wait for her to awaken. To keep her from expending her warmth on the cooling body of her mother, he took her in his arms and preserved her so till morning, as the last feeble remnant of the dead woman.

Early in the fall Voshchev began to feel the duration of time and sat indoors, surrounded by the darkness of the weary evenings.

The other men, too, either sat or lay there. The common lamp lit their faces, and no one spoke. Comrade Pashkin had providently installed a radio loudspeaker in the diggers' barrack, so that during the hours of rest each man might learn the meaning of class life.

"Comrades, we must mobilize nettles on the Socialist

construction front! Nettles are an object of necessity abroad. . . ."

"Comrades, we must clip our horses' tails and manes!" the loudspeaker demanded again. It demanded something every other minute. "Each eighty thousand horses will provide us with thirty tractors!"

Safronov listened with a sense of triumph, regretting only that he could not talk back into the speaker, to make known his readiness for all activity, for clipping horses, and his general happiness. But Zhachev, and Voshchev, too, began to feel unreasonably ashamed as they heard the long speeches over the radio. They had nothing against the speakers and admonishers, but they felt more and more acutely their personal disgrace. Sometimes Zhachev could no longer endure the oppressive despair of his soul, and he shouted amid the noise of social consciousness pouring from the loudspeaker:

"Stop that sound! Let me answer it! . . ."

Safronov would immediately step forward with his graceful walk:

"I should think, Comrade Zhachev, it's about time to give up your expressions and submit wholeheartedly to the production of the leadership."

"Leave the man alone, Safronov," Voshchev would say. "Our life is sad enough."

But the socialist Safronov was afraid of forgetting the duty of joy, and always answered everybody with finality, in the supreme voice of power:

"Whoever carries a party card in his pants pocket must be constantly concerned about keeping the enthusiasm of labor in his body. I challenge you, Comrade Voshchev, to socialist competition in the highest happiness of mood!"

The radio loudspeaker worked unceasingly, like a snowstorm, and then it proclaimed once more that every workingman must aid the accumulation of snow in the collective fields. At this, the radio fell silent; the power of science, which until then had indifferently sped across all nature the words that were so necessary to mankind, must have blown out.

Safronov, noticing the passive silence, went into action in place of the radio:

"Let us ask the question—where has the Russian people come from? And let us answer—out of bourgeois nobodies! It could have been born out of somewhere else too, but there was no more room. And this is why we must throw every man into the brine of socialism, so that the hide of capitalism will come off him, and his heart will turn its attention to the heat of life around the burning fire of class struggle, and the result will be enthusiasm!"

Having no outlet for the force of his mind, Safronov turned it into words and spoke them for a long time. Resting their heads on their hands, some listened to him, in order to fill with those sounds the empty longing in their heads; others gave themselves up to monotonous sorrow, without hearing the words and living within their personal silence. Prushevsky sat on the threshold of the barrack and looked out into the late evening of the world. He saw dark trees and heard from time to time a distant music, troubling the air. Prushevsky did not object to anything with his feelings. Life seemed good to him, when happiness was unattainable, when only the trees whispered about it, and band music sang about it in the trade union park.

Soon the entire brigade, quieted by general fatigue, fell asleep as it lived: in daytime shirts and trousers, so as not to waste strength in unbuttoning buttons, but save it for production.

Safronov alone remained without sleep. He looked at the prone men and expressed himself bitterly:

"Eh, you masses, masses. It's hard to organize the skeleton of communism out of you. And what is it you need, you vermin? Driving the whole vanguard up the wall!"

And, with a sharp sense of the wretched backwardness of the masses, Safronov huddled against one of the exhausted sleepers and sank into the dense oblivion of sleep.

In the morning, without getting up, he greeted the girl who had come with Chiklin as the element of the future, and dozed off again.

The girl cautiously sat down on a bench, discovered a map of the USSR among the slogan posters on the wall, and asked Chiklin about the meridians:

"What is that, Uncle—fences against the bourgeois?"

"They're fences, daughter, so they wouldn't climb over to us," Chiklin explained, wishing to instil in her a revolutionary mind.

"My mother never climbed over the fence, but she died anyway!"

"What can you do?" said Chiklin. "All the bourgeois women are dying now."

"Let them die," said the girl. "I remember her, anyway, and I will see her in my dreams. The only thing is, I don't have her stomach now to rest my head on when I sleep."

"Never mind, you'll sleep on my stomach," Chiklin promised.

"And now, tell me what's better—the icebreaker *Krasin* or the Kremlin?"

"That, my little one, I don't know. After all, what am I —nothing!" said Chiklin, and thought about his head, which alone in his whole body couldn't feel. If it could, he would have explained the whole world to the child, so she would know how to live safely.

The girl walked all around her new place of life and counted all objects and all people, trying to decide at once whom she liked and whom she did not like, with whom she would be friendly and with whom she wouldn't. When she was done, she was already used to the wooden barn and felt hungry.

"Give me something to eat! Hey, Julia, I'll butcher you!"

Chiklin brought her gruel and covered the child's belly with a clean towel.

"Why d'you give me cold gruel, hey, you—Julia!"

"What kind of Julia am I?"

"Oh, when my mama was called Julia, when she was still looking with her eyes and breathing all the time, she married Martynich, because he was proletarian. And Martynich, the moment he'd come in, he'd say to her, 'Hey, Julia, I'll butcher you!' And she kept quiet and went on bothering with him anyway."

Prushevsky listened and observed the girl. He had been awake for quite a while, roused by the child's appearance. It saddened him that this being, filled with fresh life as with frost, was doomed to suffering, longer and more complex than his own.

"I've found your young woman," said Chiklin to Prushevsky. "Come take a look at her, she's still whole."

Prushevsky rose and followed, for it was all the same to him—whether he was lying down or moving forward.

In the yard of the tile factory, the old man had finished his bast slippers, but he was afraid to go wandering in the world in such shoes.

"You wouldn't know, comrade, will they arrest me in bast slippers, or will they let me be?" the old man asked. "Nowadays every nobody goes strutting in leather boots. And take the women too—they wore their skirts right on their natural bodies since the world began, but now each one has flowered pants under her skirt. Isn't that something?"

"Who needs you?" said Chiklin. "Just go your way and keep your mouth shut."

"I wouldn't say a word! But here's what bothers me: they'll say—'Ah, you're in bast slippers, that means you're poor. And if you're poor, why do you live alone and don't collect yourself with the other poor? . . .' That's what I am afraid of. If not for that, I would have cleared out long ago."

"Think it over, old man," Chiklin advised him.

"Think! I've nothing left to think with anymore."

"You've lived a long life: put your memory to work."

"Eh, I've forgotten everything; looks as if there's nothing but to start life all over again from the beginning."

When they came down into the woman's refuge, Chiklin bent down and kissed her again.

"But she is dead," Prushevsky wondered.

"What of it!" said Chiklin. "Anybody can be dead if he's made to suffer enough. After all, you need her not for life, but only for remembering."

Getting down on his knees, Prushevsky touched the dead, saddened lips of the woman, and, feeling them, knew neither joy nor tenderness.

"She's not the one I saw in my youth," he said. And, getting up over the dead woman, he added: "But, then, maybe she is the one. After I felt them close, I never recognized my loved ones, but from the distance I longed for them."

Chiklin was silent. Even in strange and dead people, he felt the remnants of something warm and near to him whenever he kissed them, or somehow came into still deeper closeness to them.

Prushevsky could not bring himself to leave the dead woman. Light and ardent, she had once walked past him. He had wished himself dead at that time, seeing her walk away with lowered eyes, seeing her sad, swaying body. And after that he listened to the wind in the mournful world and longed for her. Who knows, having feared to catch up with this woman, this happiness, when he was young, he might have left her helpless, unprotected all her life, and, tired of suffering, she had hidden here, to die of hunger and of sorrow. She was lying on her back now— Chiklin had turned her to kiss her. The cord under her chin and across her head held her mouth closed. The long, bared legs were covered with thick down, almost fur, grown there from sickness and from homelessness: some ancient, reanimated force had been turning the dead woman while she was still alive into an animal, overgrowing with fur.

"Enough," said Chiklin. "Let various dead objects keep guard over her here. The dead are many, after all, like the living; they aren't lonely with their own."

And Chiklin stroked the bricks of the wall, picked up some unknown old thing and placed it next to the dead woman. Then both men went out. The woman remained lying there, in that eternal age at which she died.

After he crossed the yard, Chiklin returned and piled up broken pieces of brick, old stones and other heavy matter before the door leading to the dead woman. Prushevsky did not help him. Later he asked:

"Why are you exerting yourself?"

"What do you mean, why?" Chiklin wondered. "The dead are also people."

"But she doesn't need anything."

"She doesn't, but I need her. Let something be saved of the person. When I see the grief of the dead, or their bones, I always feel—why should I live!"

The old man who had made the bast slippers was gone from the yard; only some ragged leggings lay in his place, like a memento of the man who disappeared forever.

The sun was already high, and the hour of labor had long come. Therefore, Chiklin and Prushevsky hurried toward the foundation pit along the unpaved streets strewn with leaves which covered and kept warm the seeds of the next summer.

That evening the diggers did not switch on the loudspeaker, but, having eaten, sat down to look at the girl, thus undermining the trade union educational work over the radio. Zhachev had already resolved in the morning that as soon as this girl and others like her grew up a bit, he would finish off all the adult residents of the area. He alone knew that the USSR was populated by many total enemies of socialism, egotists and vipers of the future world, and he secretly consoled himself by the thought that one day soon he would exterminate the whole mass of them, leaving alive only proletarian infants and pure orphans.

"Who are you, little girl?" asked Safronov. "What did your father and mother do?"

"I'm nobody," the girl answered.

"How come you're nobody? Some principle of the female gender did you a favor—got you born under the Soviet government."

"I didn't want to get born—I was afraid my mother would be a bourgeois."

"Then how did you get organized?"

Confused and fearful, the girl dropped her head and started plucking at her shirt. She knew very well that she was present among the proletariat, and she guarded herself, as her mother had told her to long ago and for a long time.

"I know who's the chief man."

"Who?" Safronov listened.

"The chief one is Lenin, and the one after him, Budenny. Before they came, there were only bourgeois, and I didn't get born because I didn't want to. But as soon as Lenin came, I came too!"

"What a girl!" Safronov commented. "She was a politically conscious woman, your mother! And how deep our Soviet government is, if even children without memory of their mothers already sense Comrade Lenin!"

The unknown peasant with the yellow eyes whimpered in the corner of the barrack about the same old sorrow that troubled him, but he never said what caused it, and merely tried to please everybody as much as he could. His grieving mind imagined a village amid rye fields; a silent wind blew over it and quietly turned the wooden mill that ground out the peaceful daily bread. That was how he had lived only a short time back, his stomach filled with food and his soul with family happiness. And in all the years that he had looked out of his village into the distance and into the future, he had seen only the merging of sky and earth at the edge of the plain, and over him, the plentiful light of sun and stars.

To stop such thoughts from going on, the peasant lay down, as he always did, and hurried to weep with flowing, unpostponable tears.

"Quit your wailing, petty-bourgeois!" Safronov said to

him. "We have a child living here now. Don't you know that misery must be annulled around here?"

"I'm all dried out already, Comrade Safronov," the peasant declared from his corner. "It's my backwardness that lets my feelings get the best of me."

The girl left her seat and leaned her head against the wooden wall. She missed her mother, she was frightened of the new lonely night, and she also thought how sad it would be for her mother to lie so long, waiting till her daughter grew old and died.

"Where's the stomach?" she asked, turning to the men looking at her. "What will I sleep on?"

Chiklin lay down at once and made ready.

"And what about eating?" the girl said. "They sit there, all of them, like Julias, and I have nothing to eat!"

Zhachev rolled up to her on his platform and offered her fruit candy, which he had requisitioned that morning from the food store manager.

"Eat, poor thing! Who knows what you'll grow into; as for us, we know well enough where we are heading."

The girl ate and lay down with her face on Chiklin's stomach. She was pale with fatigue and, dozing off, she threw her arm around Chiklin as if he were her mother.

Safronov, Voshchev, and all the other diggers watched for a long time the sleep of this small being that would reign over their graves and live on a pacified earth, packed with their bones.

"Comrades!" Safronov began to articulate the general feeling. "A factual inhabitant of socialism lies before us in a state of unconsciousness. From the radio and other cultural material we hear the party line, but nothing we can touch. But here rests the substance of creation and the goal of the party—a little human being, destined to become the universal element! For that reason, we must finish the foundation pit as suddenly as possible, so that the building will rise sooner, and a stone wall will shield the childhood personnel from wind and catching colds!"

Voshchev touched the girl's hand and looked over all of her as he used to look at the angel on the church wall in his childhood. That frail little body, abandoned among people without kith or kin, would one day feel the heartwarming flow of the meaning of life, and her mind would see a time that would be like the first day of creation.

There and then the men decided to start digging the earth an hour earlier the next day, to bring nearer the laying of the rough foundation and the rest of the construction work.

"As a cripple, I can only hail your opinion, although I cannot help," said Zhachev. "You are doomed to perish anyway—your hearts are empty. Well, you had better love something little and alive, and annihilate yourselves with work. In the meantime, exist!"

In view of the chilly hour, Zhachev made the peasant take off his homespun coat and covered the child with it for the night. The peasant—he'd been accumulating capitalism all his life, he had had time enough to warm himself.

Prushevsky spent his rest days in observation, or else he wrote letters to his sister. The moment when he pasted on the stamp and dropped the letter into the mailbox always gave him a sense of quiet happiness, as though he felt someone's need for him that urged him to remain in life and labor diligently for the common good.

His sister did not write to him. She had many children and lived a careworn, almost insensible life. Only once a year, at Easter, she sent her brother a postcard, in which she reported:

> Christ has risen, my dear brother! We live as usual, I cook, the children are growing, my husband was promoted to the next grade, he now earns forty-eight rubles. Come and visit us.
>
> Your sister Anya.

Prushevsky carried the card in his pocket for a long time and sometimes cried, rereading it.

He took long walks, in solitude. Once he stopped on a hill, away from the town and the road. The day was blurred, uncertain, as though time went no further; on such days plants and animals doze, and people remember their parents. Prushevsky looked quietly at the misty, aged nature around him, and saw at its end white peaceful buildings, glowing with more light than there was in the air. He did not know the name of the completed edifices, or their purpose, although it was clear that those distant buildings were meant not only for use, but also for joy. With the astonishment of a man accustomed to sadness, Prushevsky looked at the precise delicacy and the cool, compact strength of the distant monuments. He had never seen such faith and freedom in stone laid upon stone and did not know of any self-illuminating law for the grayness of his homeland. Like an island, this white pattern of edifices stood amid the rest of the world under construction and glowed serenely. But not everything was white in those buildings. In some spots they were blue, yellow, and green, which lent them the deliberate beauty of a child's picture. "But when were they built?" Prushevsky asked with chagrin. He was more comfortable feeling sorrow on the extinct terrestrial star. Alien and distant happiness aroused within him shame and anxiety. He would have preferred, without awareness of it, that the world, eternally under construction and never finished, resemble his own ruined life.

He looked attentively again at that new city, wishing neither to forget it, nor to be mistaken, but the buildings stood there clearly and distinctly, as before, as if surrounded not by the murk of the native air, but by cool transparency.

As he returned, Prushevsky noticed many women in the city streets. The women walked slowly, despite their youth —probably strolling and awaiting the starry evening.

At dawn, Chiklin came to the office with an unknown man, dressed only in trousers.

"He wants to see you, Prushevsky," said Chiklin. "He wants the coffins for his village."

"What coffins?"

The naked man, huge, swollen from wind and grief, did not speak at once; he bowed his head first, straining to collect his thoughts. He was probably forgetting all the time to remember himself and his troubles: perhaps he was fatigued, or else dying bit by bit in the course of life.

"The coffins!" he said in a feverish, wooly voice. "We stacked the wooden coffins in the cave for future use, and you're digging up the whole ravine. We want the coffins back!"

Chiklin said that the men had indeed found a hundred empty coffins near the northern picket the day before. He had taken two of them for the girl: in one, he made a bed for her for later on, when she would start sleeping without his stomach; the other, he gave her for her toys and other childish belongings. Let her have her own little corner too.

"Give the rest of them back to the peasant," said Prushevsky.

"I want them all back," said the man. "We don't have enough dead inventory, the people are waiting for their property. We've taxed ourselves, share and share alike, to get those coffins. Don't take away what's rightfully ours!"

"No," Chiklin insisted. "Leave the two coffins for our child, they're too small for you anyway."

The unknown man stood awhile, thinking, then disagreed.

"Can't do it! Where shall we put our own children? The coffins were all built to size—they're marked, so each one will know where to go. Every man of us today lives just because he has his own coffin—that's all the property we've got now! We practiced lying in them before we hid them in the cave."

The yellow-eyed peasant who had long been living at the

foundation works hurried into the office.

"Yelisey," he said to the half-naked man. "I've tied them up with rope into a single train. Come on, we'll drag them off while the weather's still dry!"

"Couldn't keep a proper eye on them, lost two," said Yelisey reproachfully. "Where will you lie down yourself now?"

"Oh, I'll lie down, Yelisey Savvich, under the green maple in my yard, under that mighty tree. I've dug myself a hole already between the roots. I'll die, and my blood will run as sap along the trunk, it will rise way up! Or will you say my blood has gone too thin, the tree won't like the taste?"

The half-naked man stood without any impression, and did not answer. Paying no mind to the stones on the road or the chilling wind of early dawn, he went with the peasant to get the coffins. Chiklin followed them, watching Yelisey's back, covered by a whole layer of dirt of every kind and already getting overgrown with protective fur. Yelisey stopped now and then, looking into space with sleepy, emptied eyes, as if remembering the forgotten or searching for a quiet fate to give him sullen peace. But his homeland was unfamiliar to him, and he would drop his slow eyes.

The coffins stood in a long row on a dry hillock at the edge of the foundation pit. The peasant who had come running earlier to the barrack was glad that the coffins were found and that Yelisey had come. He had already managed to drill holes at the head and the foot of each coffin, and tie them up into a single harness. Yelisey took up the rope from the first coffin on his shoulder, strained forward, and dragged the wooden objects, like a river boatman, over the dry sea of life. Chiklin and the whole work brigade stood without hindrance to Yelisey and watched the furrow which the empty coffins cut in the ground.

"Uncle, were they bourgeois?" the girl asked with curiosity as she held on to Chiklin.

"No, child," Chiklin answered. "They live in straw huts, plant grain for bread, and share it half and half with us."

The girl looked up, at all the men's old faces.

"Then why do they need the coffins? Only the bourgeois must die, not the poor!"

The diggers were silent, still not knowing enough facts to answer.

"And one was naked!" said the girl. "They always take away the clothes when they're not sorry for the people, so the clothes would be saved. My mama is also lying naked."

"You are right, girl, one hundred percent," Safronov decided. "Those were two kulaks who've just left."

"Go kill them!" said the girl.

"It's not allowed, daughter. Two individuals are not a class. . . ."

"That means one, and one more," the girl counted.

"Together they were not enough," Safronov said regretfully. "And according to the plenum, we must liquidate not less than the class, so that the proletariat here and the hired village laborers would be orphaned of enemies!"

"And with whom will you be left?"

"With tasks, with the firm line of further measures—you understand?"

"Yes," the girl answered. "It means the bad people must all be killed, or else there aren't enough good ones."

"You're completely a class generation." Safronov was happy. "You are clearly conscious of all relations, even if you're just a child. It was monarchism that wanted everybody, no matter who, for war. But to us only one class is dear—and soon we'll purge our own class too of unclass-conscious elements."

"Of scum," the girl understood quickly. "Then only the chiefest, chiefest people will remain! My mama also called herself scum, when she lived, but now she died and turned good—didn't she?"

"She did," said Chiklin.

The girl, suddenly remembering that her mother lay in

darkness, walked away silently, paying no attention to anyone, and sat down to play in the sand. But she didn't play, she only touched one thing or another with an indifferent hand and thought.

The diggers went up to her and asked, bending down: "What's the matter?"

"Oh, nothing," the girl said, disregarding them. "It made me sad to be with you, you don't love me. When you fall asleep at night, I'll beat you up."

The workmen looked at one another proudly, and each wanted to take the child into his arms and feel the warm spot which generated that intelligence and the delight of that small life.

Voshchev alone stood by, feeble and joyless, mechanically looking into the distance. He still did not know whether there was anything special in the general existence—no one could read a universal set of laws to him from memory, and events on the earth's surface did not entice him. Withdrawing, Voshchev quietly moved out of sight into the field and lay down for a while, unseen by anyone, pleased that he was no longer a participant in insane situations.

Later he found the trace left by the coffins dragged away by the two peasants beyond the horizon, into their region of leaning fences overgrown with burdocks. Perhaps there was the quiet of warm places in the yards out there, or else the wretched kolkhoz poverty stood in the wind of open roads, with a pile of dead inventory in the middle. Voshchev walked in that direction, like a man mechanically dropped out from among the living, not realizing that it was only the poor cultural work at the foundation site that caused him to have no regrets about the construction of the future building. Despite the sufficiently bright sun, his heart was cheerless, especially since the fields were gray with the dizzying breath and smell of grasses. He looked around him—the mist of living breath hung over the entire landscape, creating a dazed, stifling invisibility. Wearily, patience lasted in the world, as though everything alive were somewhere in the middle of time and its own movement: its beginning was forgotten by all, and its end was unknown, nothing was left except direction. And Voshchev took the one open road.

Kozlov arrived at the foundation pit as a passenger in the car driven by Pashkin himself. Kozlov wore a light gray suit with a vest; his face had grown plump from some perpetual joy, and he had developed a great love of the proletarian masses. He began every answer to a working man with the self-contained phrase, "Very well, excellent," and then went on to speak. In his own mind he was fond of saying, "Where are you now, you miserable Fascist slut!" and many other slogan-songs.

That morning Kozlov had liquidated as a feeling his love for a certain middle-class lady. Vainly she wrote him letters about her adoration. For his part, toiling at his public tasks, he was silent, refusing in advance to confiscate her caresses, because he was looking for a woman of a nobler, more active type. Having read in the paper that the post office was overloaded and worked poorly, he decided to strengthen this sector of socialist construction by putting an end to the lady's letters to him. And he wrote her a final postcard, summing up the situation and divesting himself of the responsibility of love:

> Where formerly a laden table stood,
> There stands a coffin now!
> Kozlov

He had just read this verse and hurried not to forget it. Every day, as he awakened, he generally read books in bed and, fixing in his mind the formulations, slogans, poems, instructions, words of diverse wisdom, theses of various reports and resolutions, verses of songs, and so on, he would set out on his rounds of various government organs and institutions, where he was known and respected as an active social force. And there Kozlov intimidated the already frightened employees with his scientific approach, mental outlook, and firm grasp of principle. In addition to his first-grade pension, he thus provided himself with supplies in kind.

Entering a cooperative one day, he beckoned the manager, without moving from the spot, and said to him:

"Very well, excellent, but your cooperative, one might say, is of the Rochdale, not the Soviet type! And so, you're not a high-minded pillar on the highroad to socialism!"

"I have no precognition of you, citizen," the manager replied modestly.

"I see. So it's again: 'Passive, he sought not happiness from heaven, but daily bread, black bread, well leavened!' Very well, excellent," said Kozlov, and walked out, completely outraged. And ten days later, he became the chairman of the store committee of the cooperative. He never learned that he received this post at the request of the manager himself, who took into account not only the fiery zeal of the masses, but also the quality of the zealous.

Descending from the car, Kozlov walked to the building site with the appearance of a great mind, and stopped at the edge, for a general view of the entire tempo of the work. As for the diggers nearest to him, he said to them:

"Don't be opportunists in practice!"

During the lunch break, Comrade Pashkin informed the workmen that the poor strata of the village were mournfully longing for collective farming, and it was necessary to send there some special elements from the working class, in order to begin a class war against the remaining stumps of capitalism in the village.

"It's time we put an end to prosperous parasites!" said Safronov. "We no longer feel the heat of the bonfire of class struggle, and there must be such a fire; otherwise, where will the active personnel warm itself?"

After that, the brigade appointed Safronov and Kozlov to

go to the nearest village, so that the poor man wouldn't remain an orphan under socialism or a private swindler in his hiding place.

Zhachev rolled up to Pashkin with the girl in his cart and said to him:

"Take note of this socialism in the barefoot body. Bend down, scum, to her bones from which you've eaten off the fat!"

"A fact!" the girl confirmed.

Safronov also stated his view.

"Fix Nastya in your mind, Comrade Pashkin. Here is our future object of joy!"

Pashkin took out his notebook and placed a dot in it; there were many such dots in Pashkin's book, each denoting some fact of attention to the masses.

That evening Nastya made a separate bed for Safronov and sat down with him for a while. Safronov himself asked the girl to miss him a little, because she was the one warm-hearted woman there. And Nastya quietly stayed near him all evening, trying to think of how Safronov would go to the place where poor people languished in their huts, and how he would become louse-ridden among strangers.

Later Nastya lay down in Safronov's bed, warmed it, and left, to go to sleep on Chiklin's stomach. She had long been used to warming her mother's bed, before her second father, not her own, lay down in it.

The site for the building that would house future life was ready; the next step was the laying of the rubble base in the foundation pit. But Pashkin was forever thinking up bright thoughts, and he reported to the city chief that the projected scale of the building was too narrow, because socialist women would be full-blooded and fresh, and the whole surface of the earth would crawl with toddling infants. Could the infants, then, be left to live outside, amid unorganized weather?

"No," said the chief, accidentally elbowing a fat sandwich off the table. "Make the foundation pit four times larger."

Pashkin bent down and returned the sandwich from the floor to the table.

"It wasn't worth bending down for," said the chief. "We're planning for half a billion's worth of agricultural production in the district next year."

Pashkin put the sandwich into the tray for papers, worrying that he might be branded a man who lived by the tempos of the scarcity period.

Prushevsky awaited Pashkin near the building, to expedite the transmission of orders concerning the work. But Pashkin, as he walked along the corridor, decided to enlarge the foundation pit not by four but by six times, in order to be sure to please and get ahead of the main party line, so he could later meet it joyously in an open place. And then the line would see him and affix him in its records as an eternal dot.

"Six times larger," he instructed Prushevsky. "I told you the tempos were slow!"

Prushevsky was pleased and smiled. Noticing the engineer's delight, Pashkin was also glad, because he sensed the mood of the engineering-technical section of his union.

Prushevsky went to Chiklin, to map out the expansion of the foundation pit. Before he reached the site, he saw a crowd of diggers and a peasant wagon among the silent men. Chiklin brought an empty coffin from the barrack and placed it in the wagon; then he brought the other coffin as well, with Nastya running after him and tearing her pictures off the coffin. To pacify the girl, Chiklin lifted her up under his arm and, pressing her to himself, carried the coffin in the other arm.

"But they've died, anyway, what do they need the coffins for?" Nastya cried indignantly. "I'll have no place to put my things!"

"That's how it's got to be," Chiklin answered. "All the dead, they're special people."

"So important!" Nastya wondered. "Then why is everybody living? It would be better if they died and became important!"

"They're living so that there would be no bourgeois," said Chiklin, placing the last coffin in the wagon. In the wagon there were two men—Voshchev and the pro-kulak peasant who had once walked away with Yelisey.

"For whom are the coffins?" asked Prushevsky.

"For Safronov and Kozlov, they died in the hut, and now they're getting my coffins. What can you do?" Nastya explained in detail. And she leaned against the wagon, troubled by her loss.

Voshchev, who had arrived in the wagon from places unknown, started the horse, to return to the space where he had been. Leaving the girl in Zhachev's care, Chiklin walked at a slow pace after the wagon, drawing away into the distance.

He walked into the distance, deep into the moonlit night. From time to time small, modest lights of unknown dwellings appeared along the slope that fell away from the road, and dogs barked desolately—feeling lonely, perhaps, or frightened of official people coming into their village. The wagon with the coffins drove ahead of Chiklin all the time, and he never lost sight of it.

Leaning on the coffins with his back, Voshchev looked up from the wagon—at the starry assembly and the dead, dense blur of the Milky Way. He wondered when a resolution would be passed up there concerning discontinuation of the eternity of time and the redemption of life's weariness. Without hope, he dozed off and awakened when the wagon stopped.

Chiklin reached the wagon a few minutes later and began to look around. Nearby was an old village. The general shabbiness of poverty pervaded it; its aged, patient fences, the trees bowed silently by the roadside all had the look of sadness. All the huts in the village were lit up, but no one was outside. Chiklin went up to the first hut and struck a match to read the white piece of paper on the door. The piece of paper stated that this was the socialized house No. 7 of the General Line Kolkhoz, and that it was the home of the activist of social works aimed at fulfilling government decrees and all campaigns conducted in the village.

"Let me in!" Chiklin knocked at the door.

The activist came out and let him in. Then he prepared a receipt for the coffins and sent Voshchev to the village Soviet to stand all night as an honor guard by the bodies of the two fallen comrades.

"I'll go myself," said Chiklin.

"Go," answered the activist. "But give me your personal data, and I'll register you as a mobilized cadre."

The activist bent over his papers, his eyes carefully probing all the exact theses and assignments; with possessive greed, reckless of domestic happiness, he was building the necessary future, preparing an eternity within it for himself—and this was why he was now neglected, puffed up with cares and overgrown with scraggly hair. The lamp burned before his suspicious eyes, which mentally and factually observed the kulak vermin.

All night the activist sat by the unextinguished lamp, listening: perhaps a rider was galloping down the dark road from the district center to drop a directive on the village. He read every new directive with the curiosity of future joy, as if peeping at the passionate secrets of the grown-up, central people. There was hardly a night without a new directive, and the activist studied it, accumulating till morning the enthusiasm of unconquerable action. But often he seemed to stop dead for a moment with the anguish of life, and then he looked pitifully at any person before him: this was when he felt the recollection that he was a blunderhead and a bungler—as he was sometimes called in the papers from the district center.

Perhaps I'd better go into the masses, forget myself in the general, directed life? the activist would think to himself at those moments, but he'd quickly recover, because he did not want to be a member of the general misery and feared the long heartache of just waiting for socialism, when every shepherd would find himself in the midst of joy; for it was possible, already right now, to be a helper of the vanguard and possess immediately all the benefit of the future.

The activist spent an especially long time in studying the signatures on the papers: those letters were traced by the busy hand of the district, and a hand is a part of the whole body, which lived in plenitude of glory before the eyes of the devoted, convinced masses. Tears would actually come to his eyes as he admired the firmness of the signatures and the representations of the earth's globe on the stamps. Because the whole globe, all its softness, would soon be grasped in firm, iron hands. Could he, then, remain without any influence on the universal body of the earth? And jealously hoarding his assured future happiness, the activist stroked his chest, grown hollow in the fulfillment of his numerous tasks.

"Why are you standing there without motion?" he said to Chiklin. "Go and guard the political corpses from prosperous dishonor: you see how our heroic brothers fall!"

Through the darkness of the kolkhoz night Chiklin walked to the deserted hall of the village Soviet, where his two comrades were lying. Over the dead men burned the largest lamp, which usually illuminated meetings. They rested on the presidium table, covered with a flag up to their chins, so that the living would not see their mortal mutilations and be overcome with fear of a similar death.

Chiklin took up a position at the feet of the dead men and calmly stared at their mute faces. Safronov would never again speak out of his own mind, and Kozlov would not suffer in his heart for the entire organizational construction, and would no longer receive the pension due him.

The flowing time moved slowly in the midnight darkness of the kolkhoz; nothing disturbed its socialized property or the silence of collective consciousness. Chiklin lit a cigarette, approached the faces of the dead and touched them with his hand.

"Are you lonely, Kozlov?"

Kozlov continued to lie in silence, having been killed. Safronov was also peaceful, like a man well pleased, and his red mustache, which drooped over his weakened, half-open mouth, grew even out of his lips, because he had not been kissed while alive. Around Kozlov's and Safronov's eyes Chiklin could see the dried salt of former tears; he wiped it off and wondered—why had Safronov and Kozlov cried at the end of their lives?

"Well, Safronov, are you lying down for good, or do you think you'll get up, after all?"

Safronov could not answer, because his heart lay in a crushed breast and had no feelings.

Chiklin listened to the rain that started outside—its long, mournful sound singing in the leaves, the wattle fences, the peaceful roofs of the village. Indifferently, as if in emptiness, the fresh moisture poured down, and only the grief of even just one man, listening to the rain, could repay this exhaustion of nature. Once in a while a hen cried out in some fenced-in wilderness, but Chiklin no longer listened and lay down to sleep under the common flag between Kozlov and Safronov, because the dead were also people. The village Soviet lamp burned unsparingly over them till morning, when Yelisey came into the hall, and didn't put the lamp out, either: light and darkness were the same to him. He stood a while uselessly, and went out just as he had come.

Leaning with his chest against a flagpole stuck in the ground, Yelisey stared at the misty dampness of a vacant place. Rooks gathered in that place, preparing to fly to warm distant regions, although the time for their departure from hereabouts had not yet come. Still earlier, before the going of the rooks, Yelisey had seen the disappearance of the swallows, and he had wanted to turn into the light, hardly conscious body of a bird; but now he no longer thought of turning into a rook, because he could not think. He lived and looked with his eyes only because he had the documents of a middle peasant, and his heart was beating according to the law.

Sounds came from the village Soviet, and Yelisey went to the window and leaned toward the glass; he was constantly listening to all sounds coming from the masses, or from nature, for nobody spoke words to him and did not give him understanding, so that he had to feel even distant sounds.

Yelisey saw Chiklin sitting between two lying bodies. Chiklin was smoking and indifferently consoling the dead with his words.

"You're finished, Safronov! Well, anyway, I remain, and now I'll be like you. I'll start getting cleverer, I'll speak up with a point of view, I'll get to see your whole tendency—it's quite all right for you not to exist. . . ."

Yelisey could not understand and heard only sounds through the clear glass.

"And you, Kozlov, don't you worry about living, either. I'll forget my own self, but will keep you all the time. Your whole ruined life, all your tasks, I'll hide them inside myself and won't abandon them anywhere—so you can count yourself alive. I will be active day and night, I'll keep an eye on all organizations, I'll retire on a pension: lie in peace, Comrade Kozlov!"

Yelisey's breath made the glass foggy and he could barely see Chiklin, but he looked all the same, since he had nowhere to look. Chiklin was silent for a while, then, feeling that Safronov and Kozlov were happy now, he said to them:

"Let the whole class die—I will remain alone in its place and carry out its whole task on earth! I don't know how to live for myself anyway! . . . What's that mug staring at us? Come in, stranger!"

Yelisey immediately entered the village Soviet and stopped, not realizing that his pants had slipped down his

78

belly, although they had stayed up perfectly the day before. Yelisey had no appetite for food, and therefore got thinner every passing day.

"Was it you who killed them?" asked Chiklin.

Yelisey pulled up his pants and didn't let them go any more, saying nothing and staring at Chiklin with his pale, empty eyes.

"Who then? Go bring me somebody who kills our masses."

The peasant moved off and crossed the damp empty place where the rooks were holding their last meeting. The rooks made way for him, and Yelisey saw the peasant with the yellow eyes; he had placed a coffin against the fence and was writing his name on it in printed letters, dipping his writing finger into some thick liquid in a bottle.

"What's up, Yelisey? D'you get some new instruction?"

"Mm. . . . Nothing," said Yelisey.

"Then it's all right," the writing peasant said calmly. "Were the dead in the Soviet washed yet? I'm afraid the public invalid might come in his cart. He'll let me have it, because I'm alive and the two are dead."

The peasant went to wash the corpses, so as to reveal his concern and sympathy. Yelisey tagged along, not knowing where it was best to be.

Chiklin made no objection while the peasant took the clothes off the murdered men and carried them naked, one after the other, to dip them in the pond. Then, drying them well with a sheepskin, he dressed them again and put both bodies on the table.

"All right, fine," said Chiklin after that. "And who killed them?"

"That isn't known to us, Comrade Chiklin—we ourselves live just by accident."

"By accident!" Chiklin said, and hit the peasant in the face, so he'd live consciously. The peasant fell, but he was afraid to move back too far, or Chiklin might think something prosperous about him, and he stood up even closer to him, hoping to get maimed still worse, and earn by his suffering the right to life as a poor man. Seeing such a creature before him, Chiklin mechanically pushed his fist into his belly, and the peasant toppled backward, closing his yellow eyes.

Yelisey, who stood quietly at the side, told Chiklin soon afterwards that the peasant wasn't moving.

"Why, are you sorry for him?" asked Chiklin.

"No," said Yelisey.

"Put him down in the middle between my comrades."

Yelisey dragged the peasant toward the table and, straining his whole body, lifted him and dropped him across the former corpses; then he fitted him in properly, squeezing him in tightly between the sides of Safronov and Kozlov. When Yelisey stepped away, the peasant opened his yellow eyes, but could no longer close them, and so remained staring.

"Has he got a woman?" Chiklin asked Yelisey.

"He was alone," Yelisey answered.

"Then why'd he live?"

"He was afraid of not living."

Voshchev came in the door and told Chiklin to come—the *activ* wanted him.

"Here's a ruble." Chiklin hurriedly gave Yelisey the money. "Go to the foundation pit and see if the girl Nastya is alive, and buy her some candy. My heart's begun to ache for her."

The activist sat with his three assistants, lean from continual heroism and entirely poor men, but their faces expressed the same firm feeling—zealous devotion. The activist informed Chiklin and Voshchev that, according to Comrade Pashkin's directive, they must adapt all their hidden forces to the service of kolkhoz development.

"What about the truth, is the proletariat supposed to get it?" asked Voshchev.

"The proletariat's supposed to move," the activist pronounced. "And whatever comes its way—it might be the truth, or it might be the kulak's looted blouse—belongs to the proletariat; it all goes into the organized cauldron, you will not recognize anything."

Sitting near the dead in the village Soviet, the activist at first felt sad, but then, recalling the new future they were building, he smiled with energy and ordered those around him to mobilize the kolkhoz for a funeral procession, so that everyone would feel the solemnity of death during the time of the developing bright moment of socialization of property.

Kozlov's left arm hung down, and his whole ruined body leaned over the edge of the table, ready to fall unconsciously. Chiklin righted him and noticed that the dead were altogether crowded now: there were four of them instead of three. He did not remember the fourth one, and he turned to the activist for enlightenment concerning the misfortune, although the fourth was not a proletarian but some dull peasant, lying crookedly on his side, with silenced breath. The activist reported to Chiklin that this propertied element was the mortal wrecker of Safronov and Kozlov; but then he had realized his grief over the organized movement against him, so he came in himself, lay down between the dead, and personally died.

"I would have discovered him in half an hour anyway," said the activist. "We haven't got any elemental forces now, there's no place for a man to hide! But I see an extra one lying here too."

"I finished that one," Chiklin explained. "I figured the bastard came here begging for a blow. I poked him, but he was too weak."

"Right: they wouldn't believe me in the district that there was just one killer, but two—that's already a whole kulak class and organization!"

After the funeral, the sun went down on one side of the kolkhoz, and immediately the world turned desolate and alien. A dense underground cloud rose from the morning edge of the region; by midnight it would reach the local fields and spill on them its full weight of cold water. Looking at it, the kolkhoz peasants began to feel chilly; and the hens were clucking in their coops, in premonition of the long autumn night. Soon solid darkness descended on the earth, deepened by the blackness of the soil, trampled down by the wandering masses. But up above it was still light. Amid the damp inaudible wind high overhead the yellow glow of the sun that reached it lingered and was reflected on the last foliage of the silent, bowed orchards. People did not want to be inside their huts, where they were attacked by thoughts and moods; they wandered all over the open places of the village, trying constantly to see each other. They also listened keenly for any sound coming from the distance through the damp air, hoping to hear some consolation in such difficult space. The activist had long ago issued an oral directive to observe sanitary rules in social life, meaning that people should be outside all the time instead of suffocating in their family huts. This made it easier for the *activ*, as it met, to keep an eye on the masses from the window and to lead them ever forward.

The activist had also noticed the yellow sunset, resembling the light of burial, and resolved on the very next morning to announce a starlight march of the kolkhoz members to nearby villages that still clung to private ownership, and then to declare a series of popular games.

The chairman of the village Soviet, a little old middle peasant, went up to the activist for instructions, because he was afraid of doing nothing, but the activist retired him from himself with his hand, saying only that the village Soviet must consolidate the hind victories of the *activ* and guard the ruling poor from kulak sharks. The little old chairman was gratefully reassured and went off to make himself a watchman's rattle.

Voshchev was afraid of nights—he lay in them without sleep and doubted. His basic sense of life strove for something fitting in the world, and the hidden hope of thought promised him distant salvation from the incomprehensibility of general existence. He went with Chiklin to their lodging for the night and worried that the other would immediately lie down and fall asleep, while he would be alone, staring with his eyes into the darkness over the kolkhoz.

"Don't sleep tonight, Chiklin. I'm somehow afraid."

"Don't be afraid. Tell me who frightens you—I'll kill him."

"I'm afraid of perplexity of heart, Comrade Chiklin. I don't know myself what it is. It seems to me all the time that there is something special in the distance, or some splendid unattainable object, and I live in sadness."

"Oh, we'll get it. Don't worry, as they say, Comrade Voshchev."

"When, Comrade Chiklin?"

"Consider that it has been gotten already: see how everything's become nothing now. . . ."

At the edge of the kolkhoz there was an Organizational Yard, in which the activist and other leading poor peasants conducted the education of the masses. It was also the place where unproved kulaks lived, and various other guilty members of the collective. Some of them were in the Orgyard for falling into the petty mood of doubt; others for crying during the time of optimism and kissing the fenceposts in their yards, which were being socialized; still others for something else; and, finally, there was an old man who had come to the Orgyard spontaneously: he was the watchman of the tile factory, on his way somewhere across the yard when he'd been stopped because of an alien expression on his face.

Voshchev and Chiklin sat down on a stone in the middle of the yard, intending to go to sleep soon under the shed. The old man from the tile factory remembered Chiklin and came up to him. Until then, he had been sitting in the nearby grass, rubbing the dirt off his body under the shirt without using water.

"Why are you here?" asked Chiklin.

"Oh, I was walking, and they told me to stop here. Maybe you shouldn't be living, they said, we have to see. I tried to go by, saying nothing, but they turned me back: Halt, they shouted, you kulak creature! Ever since then I've been here, living on potatoes."

"What's the difference to you where you live," said Chiklin. "So long as you don't die."

"True enough! I can get used to anything, it's only hard in the beginning. They've taught me letters here, and now it's numbers they want me to know. You'll be a proper class-conscious old man, they say. Well, why not—I will, too!"

The old man was ready to talk all night, but Yelisey returned from the foundation pit and brought Chiklin a letter from Prushevsky. Under the lamp that lit up the sign of the Orgyard, Chiklin read that Nastya was alive, and that Zhachev began to take her daily to nursery school, where she learned to love the Soviet government and began collecting trash for reuse. Prushevsky himself felt very sad about the killing of Kozlov and Safronov, and Zhachev cried for them with huge tears.

Comrade Prushevsky wrote:

> It's pretty hard for me, and I am afraid I'll fall in love with some woman and marry her, since I have no social significance. The foundation pit is ready. In the spring we'll lay the rubble filler. Nastya, it turns out, can write in printed letters, I am enclosing her message.

Nastya wrote to Chiklin:

> Liquidate the kulak as a class. Long live Lenin, Kozlov, and Safronov!
> Regards to the poor kolkhoz, but not to the kulaks.

Chiklin whispered these words for a long time, and was deeply moved, not knowing how to wrinkle his face for sorrow and tears. Then he went to sleep.

In the big house of the Organizational Yard there was one enormous room, and everybody slept there on the floor, because of the cold. Forty or fifty people opened their mouths and breathed upward, and under the low ceiling a lamp hung in a haze of sighs and swayed quietly from the shaking of the ground. Yelisey lay in the middle of the floor; his sleeping eyes were almost entirely open and looked without blinking at the burning lamp. Finding Voshchev, Chiklin lay down next to him and rested till the brighter morning.

In the morning the barefoot kolkhoz marchers lined up in a row in the Orgyard. Each of them had a flag with a slogan in his hand and a bag with food over his shoulder. They waited for the activist, as the primary man in the kolkhoz, to learn from him why they had to go to strange places.

The activist came into the yard together with the leading personnel and, arranging the marchers in the shape of a five-cornered star, he took up his position in the center and spoke his word, instructing the marchers to go among the surrounding poor and show them the nature of a kolkhoz by calling them to socialist order, because later it would be bad anyway. Yelisey held the longest flag in his hands, and, meekly hearing out the activist, he started forward in his customary walk, not knowing where he must stop.

The morning was damp, and cold air blew from distant empty places. This circumstance was not overlooked by the *activ.*

"Sabotage!" the activist said gloomily about the chilling wind of nature.

The poor and middle peasants went out upon their journey and disappeared far off, in outside space. Chiklin followed the departing barefoot collectivization with his eyes, and did not know what to suppose next. Voshchev was

85

silent, without thinking. A wall of rain came down from the huge cloud which stopped over deserted distant fields and covered the vanished marchers with moisture.

"Where did they go, anyway?" asked one kulak, isolated from the population of the Organizational Yard for his harmfulness. The activist had forbidden him to go beyond the fence, and the kulak expressed himself through it. "We have enough shoes for ten years, so where do they think they're going?"

"Let him have it," Chiklin said to Voshchev.

Voshchev went up to the kulak and hit him in the face. The kulak did not speak again.

Voshchev approached Chiklin with his usual puzzlement about surrounding life.

"Look, Chiklin, how the kolkhoz goes out into the world —barefoot and sad."

"That's why they go, because they're barefoot," said Chiklin. "And they've nothing to be happy about—after all, the kolkhoz is a matter of daily life."

"Christ must have gone about sadly too, and there was miserable rain in nature."

"You've got no brains," answered Chiklin. "Christ went about alone, who knows for what, and here whole mobs are moving for the sake of existence."

The activist stayed where he was, in the Orgyard. The previous night had been a waste—no directive had dropped on the kolkhoz, and he let thoughts flow in his own head. But thinking brought him fear of oversights. He was afraid that prosperity would be accumulated in the private households, and he would fail to notice. At the same time he was afraid of excessive zeal. Therefore, he socialized only the horses, tormenting himself over the lonely cows, sheep, and fowl, because in the hands of the uncontrolled private owner even a goat was a lever of capitalism.

Restraining the force of his initiative, the activist stood motionless amid the general silence of the kolkhoz, and his assistant comrades looked at his stilled lips, not knowing where to go next. Chiklin and Voshchev left the Orgyard and went to look for dead inventory, so as to judge its fitness.

After walking some distance, they halted on the way, because on the right side of the street a gateway opened without human effort and calm horses began to come out of it. In an even step, not lowering their heads to the food growing on the ground, the horses passed the street in a compact mass and went down to the ravine, which held water. Having drunk their normal portion, the horses entered the water and stood in it for a while for the sake of cleanliness; then they came up to the dry land of the bank and started back, without breaking formation and solidarity. At the first houses, however, the horses dispersed. One stopped by a straw roof and began to tug at the straw; another bent down and collected in its mouth tufts of meager remnants of hay; the more sullen horses entered the farmsteads, took sheaves from their old, familiar places, and brought them out into the street.

Every animal picked up a share of food according to its capacity and brought it carefully to the gates from which all the horses had come out before.

The horses that came first stopped at the common gateway and waited for the rest of the equine mass, and when all of them had assembled together, the horse in front pushed the gates open with its head, and the entire formation entered the yard with the fodder. In the yard, the horses opened their muzzles, and the fodder dropped into a single pile. Then the socialized livestock gathered around the pile and slowly began to eat, organizationally reconciled to living without man's care.

Voshchev looked at the animals in fright through a crack in the gate; he was astonished at the spiritual serenity of the chewing animals, as if all the horses were completely convinced of the kolkhoz meaning of life, and he alone lived and suffered more than a horse.

Beyond the horses' yard stood someone's ramshackle hut

on a naked spot of land, without field or fence. Chiklin and Voshchev entered the hut and noticed a peasant lying face down on a bench. His woman was sweeping the floor. Seeing the guests, she wiped her nose with a corner of her kerchief, which released a customary flood of tears.

"What's the matter?" Chiklin asked her.

"O-o-oh, my doves!" the woman said and cried still harder.

"Hurry up, dry out and speak!" Chiklin reasoned with her.

"My man's been lying there for days and days. . . . Stuck himself to the bench. 'Woman,' he says, 'stuff some food in my innards, I'm all empty lying here, my soul is gone from my whole flesh, I'm afraid I'll fly off. Put down some weight on my shirt,' he yells. As soon as evening comes, I tie a samovar to his belly. When are we going to see some life?"

Chiklin went up to the peasant and turned him face up. He was really very thin and light, and his petrified pale eyes expressed nothing, not even fear. Chiklin bent down over him.

"What's with you? Are you breathing?"

"When I remember, I take a breath," the man answered weakly.

"And what if you forget to breathe?"

"Then I'll die."

"Maybe you do not feel the sense of life. Endure and wait a while," Voshchev said to the prostrate peasant.

The man's wife stealthily but closely examined the guests, and the bitterness of her eyes insensibly dried her tears.

"He knew everything, Comrades, he saw everything through and through in his heart! But when they took away our horse into the organization, he lay down and just stopped. I can cry at least, he can't."

"Better let him cry, be easier for him," Voshchev advised.

"I told him. Can a man lie silently? The government will be scared. As for me—and that's the whole truth—you seem to be good men, the moment I come out in the street, I cry my eyes out, in front of all the people. And the comrade activist sees me—he looks all over, you know, he's counted every splinter of wood—he sees me and he orders: 'Cry, woman, cry as hard as you can. It's the sun of the new life that has risen, and the light hurts your ignorant eyes.' And his voice is steady and even, and I see that nothing will be done to me, and I cry with all my might. . . ."

"So your man's been living only lately without spiritual zeal?" asked Voshchev.

"Oh, ever since he stopped knowing me as his wife, I guess that's when it started."

"His soul is a horse," said Chiklin. "Let him live empty a while, the wind will blow through him."

The woman opened her mouth, but remained soundless, because Voshchev and Chiklin went out of the door.

Another house stood on a large farmstead, surrounded by fences. Inside, a peasant lay in an empty coffin, and at every sound he shut his eyes, as if dead. An icon lamp had been burning at the head of the half-sleeping man for several weeks, and from time to time the coffin's tenant added oil to it from a bottle. Voshchev leaned his hand against the dead man's forehead and felt that the man was warm. The peasant heard and stopped his breath altogether, trying to cool off as much as he could outside. He clenched his teeth and let no air into his depths.

"He's colder now," said Voshchev.

The peasant strained his whole dim strength to stop the internal pulsing of his life, but, after many years of running, life could not stop in him. Look at that strength that cares for me inside me, the prone man thought between efforts. But wait, I'll get you, anyway, you'd better stop by your own self.

"Seems to have gotten warmer," Voshchev discovered after a time.

"That means he's not afraid yet, the kulak element," said Chiklin.

The peasant's heart rose independently into his soul, into the tight space of his throat, and shrank there, letting out the heat of dangerous life into the upper skin. He moved his feet to help his heart to give a start, but the heart by now was all worn out without air and could not work. The peasant opened wide his mouth and screamed from grief and death, pitying his intact bones for rotting into dust, the bloody strength of his body for putrefaction, his eyes for the disappearing light of the world, and his house for being eternally orphaned.

"The dead make no noise," Voshchev said to the peasant.

"I won't," the man agreed and lay still, happy that he had pleased the government.

"He's getting cold," Voshchev said, feeling the peasant's neck.

"Put out the lamp," said Chiklin. "The fire burns over him, and he shut his eyes against it. There is no economy here for the sake of the revolution."

As they came out into the fresh air, Chiklin and Voshchev met the activist—he was on the way to the reading-room hut on affairs of the cultural revolution. After that, it was his duty to make the rounds of all the middle private householders who remained outside the kolkhoz, in order to persuade them of the senselessness of fenced-in household capitalism.

In the reading room stood previously organized kolkhoz women and girls.

"Hello, Comrade *activ!*" they said all together.

"Greetings to the cadre!" the activist replied pensively, and stood a while in silent thought. "And now we shall repeat the letter 'A'—listen to my words and write. . . ."

The women lay down on the floor, because the whole reading room was empty, and began to write on boards with bits of plaster. Chiklin and Voshchev also sat down on the floor, wishing to strengthen their knowledge of the ABC's.

"What words begin with 'A'?" asked the activist.

One happy girl rose to her knees and answered with the full brightness and quickness of her mind:

"Avant-garde, *activ*, amen-sayers, advance, arch-leftist, antifascist!"

"Right, Makarovna," the activist approved. "Now write these words systematically."

The women and the girls diligently leaned over the floor and stubbornly began to draw the letters, scraping with their pieces of plaster. The activist meanwhile gazed out of the window, deliberating about some further move, or perhaps suffering from his lonely class-consciousness.

"Why are they writing the hard-ending sign?"* asked Voshchev.

The activist turned to him.

"Because words make up party lines and slogans, and a hard-ending sign is much more useful than a soft-ending one. It's the soft that ought to be abolished, but the hard is inevitable to us: it makes for harshness and clarity of formulations. Does everybody understand?"

"Yes, everybody," said everybody.

"Now write words starting with 'B'. Speak, Makarovna!"

Makarovna raised herself and spoke, with confidence in science:

"Bolshevik, bourgeois, bump, back the chairman, the kolkhoz benefits the poor, bravo, bravo, Leninists!"

"You forgot bureaucracy," commented the activist.

*TRANSLATOR'S NOTE: In pre-revolutionary orthography, every word ending with a consonant was concluded with a sign indicating a hard or a soft sound. After the revolution, the alphabet was reformed: several letters duplicating the same sound and complicating spelling were abolished, as was the hard-ending sign.

"Well, write the words. And you, Makarovna, run over to the church and light my pipe."

"Let me go," said Chiklin. "Don't divert people from intelligence."

The activist filled the pipe with chopped burdock leaves, and Chiklin went to light it with fire. The church stood at the edge of the village, and beyond it began the desolateness of autumn and the eternal acquiescence of nature. Chiklin looked at that destitute silence, at the distant willows in the chilling, clayey fields, but could find no words as yet to protest.

Near the church grew old forgotten grass, and there were no paths or other traces of human feet; evidently, people had not prayed in the church for a long time. Chiklin walked through the dense thicket of goosefoot and burdocks, and stepped upon the porch. There was no one on the cool porch—only a huddled sparrow lived in the corner. It was not frightened of Chiklin, but merely looked at the man silently, probably preparing to die soon in the darkness of autumn.

Many candles burned inside the church; the light of the silent, mournful wax illuminated the entire interior, up to the ceiling beneath the cupola, and the clean faces of saints looked at the dead air with an expression of indifference, like residents of the other, peaceful world, but the church was empty.

Chiklin lit the pipe from the nearest candle and noticed someone else smoking near the ambo. He saw a man sitting on the step on the ambo, smoking. Chiklin went up to him.

"You've come from the activist comrade?" the smoker asked.

"What's that to you?"

"I can tell by the pipe, anyway."

"And who are you?"

"I was a priest, but now I've cut myself off from my soul and had my hair shorn in the foxtrot cut. See?"

The priest removed his cap and showed Chiklin a head, barbered like a girl's.

"Not bad, eh? . . . But they don't believe me anyway. They say I'm a secret believer and an open viper to the poor. I've got to earn my status, so they'll accept me in the Godless circle."

"And how do you earn it, you scum?" asked Chiklin.

The priest put away his bitterness into his heart and answered readily:

"Oh, I sell candles to the people—see how the whole place is lit up! The money's collected in the cup and turned over to the activist for a tractor."

"Stop bluffing: where are the pious folk around here?"

"There can't be any here," the priest said. "People just buy candles and light them, like orphans, as an offering to God instead of prayers. Then they leave right away."

Chiklin took a deep, angry breath and asked again:

"Then why don't people cross themselves here, you rotter?"

The priest rose to his feet before him as a sign of respect, preparing to give an exact answer.

"It's not permissible to cross yourself here, Comrade. If someone does, I enter his name in speedwriting in the memorial list. . . ."

"Go on, make it fast!" ordered Chiklin.

"I haven't stopped telling, Comrade Brigadier, though I'm not quite up to tempos, just bear with me . . . I bring the lists with the indication of those who made the sign of the cross with their hand, or bowed their body before the heavenly power, or committed any other act of worship of the kulak saints—I bring them every midnight personally to the activist comrade."

"Come up closer to me," said Chiklin.

The priest readily came down from the ambo steps.

"Close your eyes, vermin."

The priest closed his eyes, with an expression of heartfelt

93

amiability on his face. Chiklin, without stirring his body, delivered a class-conscious punch to the priest's face. The priest opened his eyes and closed them again, but couldn't let himself fall for fear of giving Chiklin the idea that he was insubordinate.

"You want to live?" asked Chiklin.

"Living's no use to me," the priest answered sensibly. "I no longer feel the beauty of creation—I'm left without God, and God's without man. . . ."

After the last words, the priest bowed down to the ground and began to pray to his guardian angel, touching the floor with his head, shorn in the foxtrot style.

A long whistle came from the village, followed by the neighing of horses.

The priest halted his praying hand and figured out the meaning of the signal.

"A founder's meeting," he said meekly.

Chiklin went out of the church and into the grass. A peasant woman walked through the grass toward the church, straightening up the trampled goosefoot behind her. But seeing Chiklin she froze with fright and held out to him five kopeks for a candle.

The Organizational Yard was solidly filled with people; the organized members and the unorganized private peasants, those who were still weak in class-consciousness or who were close to a kulak way of life and did not join the kolkhoz.

The activist stood on the high stoop and observed the movement of the living mass on the damp evening earth with silent sadness. He loved the poor who, having eaten their coarse bread, eagerly strove forward into the bright future, for the earth was empty and full of disquiet for them anyway. He secretly gave candy from the city to the children of the landless, and had decided to aim at marriage when communism came to the village, especially since the quality of women was bound to improve then. And now someone's little child stood near the activist and looked up at his face.

"What're you staring at?" asked the activist. "Here, have a piece of candy."

The boy took the candy, but food alone was not enough for him.

"Uncle, how come you're the smartest, but you have no cap?"

The activist patted the boy's head without answering. The child bit through the solid, pebblelike candy with wonder; it glittered like split ice, and there was nothing inside it except its hardness. The boy returned half of the candy to the activist.

"Finish it yourself, it has no jam inside; not much pleasure in it!"

The activist smiled with penetrating awareness; he sensed that this child would remember him in the maturity of his life amid the burning light of socialism, obtained from the fenced yards of the villages by the concerted strength of the *activ*.

Voshchev and three other convinced peasants carried logs to the gates of the Orgyard and stacked them there. The activist had assigned them to this task beforehand.

Chiklin joined the working men, and, picking up a log in the ravine, carried it to the Orgyard: let there be more benefit for the common good, so it wouldn't be so sad all around.

"Well, what's it going to be, citizens?" the activist said into the substance of the people gathered before him. "Are you, then, planning to sow capitalism again, or have you come to your senses?"

The organized men sat down on the ground and smoked with a satisfactory feeling, stroking their beards, which for some reason had thinned out in the past half-year. The unorganized stood on their feet, struggling with their futile souls, but one of the *activ*'s assistants had taught them that they had no souls, nothing but propertied inclinations, and now they didn't know altogether how it would be with them when there was no more property. Others bent their heads and struck at their breasts, listening to their thoughts from there; but their hearts beat lightly and sorrowfully, as if empty, and gave no answer. The standing men didn't take their eyes off the activist for a moment, and those closest to the porch looked at the man in charge with complete willingness in their unblinking eyes, so he would see their readiness of mood.

By that time, Chiklin and Voshchev had finished the delivery of logs and began to hew the ends for dovetailing, trying to build some large object. There was no sun in nature that day, or the previous day, and the dreary evening fell early over the wet fields. Quiet was spreading now over the entire visible world; only Chiklin's axe was heard in it, echoed by the decrepit creaking of the fences and the nearby mill.

"Well!" the activist said patiently from above. "Or do you mean to keep on standing there between capitalism and communism? It's time to get moving—we've got the fourteenth plenum going in the district!"

"Let us middle peasants stand here a bit longer, Comrade *activ*," begged the peasants in the rear. "Maybe we'll get used to things: habit's the main thing with us, after that we can put up with anything."

"All right, stand while the poor are sitting," the activist gave his permission. "Anyway, Comrade Chiklin hasn't finished hammering the logs together into a single block yet."

"And what are they being fitted together for, Comrade *activ?*" asked one of the middle peasants in the rear.

"They're being organized into a raft for the liquidation of classes. Tomorrow the kulak sector will float down the river to the sea, and farther on. . . ."

Taking out the memorial lists and the class-stratification document, the activist began to make marks on the papers; he had a multicolored pencil, and sometimes he used the blue, sometimes the red color. Or else he simply sighed and pondered, without writing down the marks before making up his mind. The standing peasants opened their mouths and gaped at the pencil with torment in their feeble souls, which—seeing as they started hurting—must have appeared inside them out of the last remnants of their private property. Chiklin and Voshchev worked with their two axes at once, and the logs fitted close to one another, making roomy space above.

The nearest middle peasant leaned his head on the porch and stood in that immobility a while.

"Comrade *activ*, say, Comrade!"

"Speak clearly," the activist, busy with other things, said to the peasant.

"Allow us to grieve over our trouble for one remaining night, then we'll be happy with you for the rest of our lives!"

The activist thought briefly.

"A night's a long time. Around us tempos are moving all over the district. You can grieve until the raft is ready."

"Well, at least until the raft, that's a joy too," said the middle peasant and began to cry, to lose none of the time for the final grief. The peasant women standing outside the Orgyard fence wailed in chorus with choked voices, so that Chiklin and Voshchev stopped hewing the wood with their axes. The organized poor got up from the ground, glad that they didn't have to grieve, and went off to examine the common, essential property of the village.

"Turn away from us for a while too," three middle peasants begged the activist. "Let's not see you."

The activist withdrew from the porch and went into the house, where he avidly began to write a report about the exact fulfillment of the measure for total collectivization and the liquidation of the kulaks as a class by means of floating them downriver on a raft. The activist could not put a comma after the word "kulaks," since there was no comma in the directive, either. He went on to ask the district to assign him a new militant campaign, so that the local *activ* could work without interruption and clearly carry the beloved general line forward. The activist also would have liked the district center to name him in its resolution the most ideological worker of the entire district superstructure, but this desire died down in him without consequences because he remembered himself saying, after the grain collection, that he was the cleverest man at the given stage of sowing, upon which a peasant who heard him declared himself a woman, not a man.

The door of the house opened and let in the noise of torment from the village; the new arrival wiped the wetness from his clothes and said:

"Comrade *activ*, it's snowing out there, and a cold wind's blowing."

"Let it snow, what's it to us?"

"To us it's nothing, we can manage whatever comes!" the elderly poor peasant agreed readily. He was constantly amazed that he was still alive, because he had nothing except vegetables from his little garden and the privileges granted to the poor, and could never attain a higher, easier life.

"Tell me, Comrade chief, console my heart: shall I join the kolkhoz for peace and quiet, or shall I wait?"

"Join it, naturally, or I'll send you to the ocean."

"A poor man isn't scared of anyplace; I would have joined up long ago, except that Zoya shouldn't be planted."

"What Zoya? If you mean soya, it's an official crop!"

"That's her, the bitch."

"Well, don't plant it—I'll make allowance for your psychology."

"Please do."

After he registered the poor peasant as a member of the kolkhoz, the activist was obliged to give him a note attesting to his admission to membership and promising that there would be no Zoya in the kolkhoz; he had to devise the proper form for such a statement, for the man refused to leave without it.

Meantime, the cold snow outside fell more and more densely. The snow quieted the earth, but the sounds of the middle peasants' mood prevented total silence. The old plowman Ivan Semyonovich Krestyanin kissed the young trees in his orchard and wrenched them out of the soil with the roots, and his wife keened over the bare branches.

"Stop crying, old woman," said Krestyanin. "In the kolkhoz you'll become a muzhiks' whore. But these trees are my own flesh, so let it suffer now, it hates to be socialized into bondage."

Hearing the man's words, the woman rolled upon the ground. Another woman—an old maid or a widow—ran along the street, wailing in such a nunlike, propagandist voice that Chiklin felt like shooting her; then she saw Krestyanin's wife rolling below, and she also flung herself down and began to bang her feet in cotton stockings on the ground.

Night covered the whole village, the snow made the air impenetrable and close, stopping all breath, but yet the women cried out everywhere and, growing accustomed to misery, kept up a constant howl. The dogs and other small, nervous creatures echoed those tormenting sounds, and the kolkhoz was as noisy and troubled as a bathhouse dressing room. And all the time, the middle and the richer peasants worked silently in the yards and barns, guarded by the women's wailing at the wide-open gates. The remaining unsocialized horses slept sadly in their stalls, tied firmly to them so they wouldn't drop, and some of the standing horses were already dead. In expectation of the kolkhoz, the more prosperous peasants kept their horses without feed, so nothing but their own bodies would be socialized, and they wouldn't have to lead their livestock with them into sorrow.

"Still alive, darling?"

The mare dozed in the stall, her keen head lowered forever; one eye was partly closed, but she hadn't had strength enough to close the other, and it stared into the dark. The stable got chilled without the mare's breath; snow drifted in, fell on the mare's head and did not melt. Her master blew out the candle, put his arm around her neck, and stood in wretched solitude, smelling, by old habit, the mare's sweat, as at plowing time.

"So you've died? Well, no matter—I'll die too before long, it will be peaceful for us."

A dog came into the stable, not seeing the man, and sniffed at the horse's hind leg. Then it growled, sank its teeth into the flesh, and pulled out a piece of meat. Both of the mare's eyes glowed white in the darkness, she looked with both, and moved her feet a step forward, still remembering to live when feeling pain.

"Maybe you'll join the kolkhoz? Go on, then, and I will wait a while," said the master.

He took a tuft of hay from the corner and brought it to the horse's mouth. But the mare's eyesockets were dark now, she had already shut out her last sight and did not feel the smell of grass, because her nostrils no longer quivered at the hay, and two other dogs indifferently fed on her hind leg. But the horse's life was still intact—it merely shrank in distant poverty, broke up into continually smaller particles, and could not weary itself out.

Snow fell on the cold earth, preparing to remain into the winter; a peaceful blanket covered all visible ground for its coming sleep. The snow melted only around the barns, and the earth was black there, because the blood of cows and sheep seeped out from beneath the walls, and summer places were bared. Having liquidated the last of their steaming live inventory, the peasants began to eat meat and ordered their entire households to eat it too. During that brief time eating meat was like Communion. Nobody wanted to eat, but it was necessary to hide the flesh of the butchered family beasts inside one's body and save it there from socialization. Some cunning peasants had long grown bloated from the meat diet and walked heavily, like moving barns. Others vomited continually, but they could not part from their livestock and devoured it to the bone, without expecting to benefit their stomachs. Those who had managed to finish their livestock, and those who had let it go into kolkhoz captivity, lay down in their empty coffins and lived in them as in their own narrow homes, feeling sheltered and at rest.

Chiklin halted work on the raft. Voshchev, too, became so enfeebled in body without ideology that he could not lift the axe and lay down in the snow: there was no truth in the world anyway, or, perhaps, it had existed in some plant or some heroic creature, but a wayside beggar passed by and ate that plant or trampled the low-bending creature, then died himself in an autumn ravine, and the wind blew his body to nothing.

The activist saw from the Orgyard that the raft wasn't ready. However, he had to send a packet with his summary report to the district center the next morning; therefore, he blew his whistle for a general constituent assembly. The people came out of the yards in answer to this sound and gathered in a still unorganized crowd on the site of the Orgyard. The women were no longer crying and their faces had dried out, the men also carried themselves self-obliviously, prepared to organize for eternity. The people came close together and the whole middle mass stared wordlessly at the porch, where the activist stood with a lantern in his hand; because of his own light, he could not see the various trifles in the faces of the people, but he himself was observed quite clearly.

"Are you ready?" asked the activist.

"Wait," said Chiklin to the activist. "Let them say good-bye until the future life."

The peasants prepared for something, but one of them spoke up amid the silence: "Give us another moment of time!"

And with those last words, the peasant embraced his neighbor, kissed him three times and bade him farewell.

"Farewell, Yegor Semyonych, and forgive me!"

"Nothing to forgive, Nikanor Petrovich; forgive me too."

Everyone began to kiss the whole line of people, embracing hitherto strange bodies, and all lips sadly and lovingly kissed all others.

"Farewell, Aunt Darya, don't hold it against me that I burned down your threshing barn."

"God will forgive you, Alyosha—the barn isn't mine now, anyway."

Many, touching mutual lips, stood in this feeling for a while, in order to remember forever their new kin, because until then they had lived without remembering one another and without pity.

"Well, let's be brothers, Stepan."

"Good-bye, Yegor—we lived in enmity, but we end in good conscience."

After the kissing, the people bowed low to the ground, each to all, and rose to their feet free and with empty hearts.

"We're ready now, Comrade *activ*. Write us all down in one column, and we ourselves will show you the kulaks."

But the activist had already marked off all the village residents before—some into the kolkhoz, some for the raft.

"So consciousness has spoken up in you!" he said. "I guess the *activ*'s mass work has had its effect! There it is, the clear line and the future light!"

Chiklin came up on the high porch and put out the activist's lantern—the night was bright enough from the fresh snow without kerosene.

"Are you happy now, comrades?" asked Chiklin.

"We are," came back from the whole Orgyard. "We don't feel nothing now, there is nothing but ashes left inside us."

Voshchev lay at the side and could not fall asleep without the peace of truth within his life. He rose from the snow and went among the people.

"Hello!" he said to the kolkhoz joyously. "You have become like me—I'm also nothing."

"Hello!" the entire kolkhoz rejoiced to welcome one man.

Chiklin could not endure being separate on the porch when all the people stood together below; he came down on the ground, made a fire of the fence material, and everyone started warming up around the flames.

The night hung murkily over the people, and nobody spoke any more; the only sound was a dog's barking from some distant village, the same as in the olden times, as if the animal existed in a permanent eternity.

Chiklin awakened first, because something important came to his mind, but when he opened his eyes, he forgot everything. Before him stood Yelisey with Nastya in his arms. He had held the girl for almost two hours, afraid to rouse Chiklin, and she slept quietly, warm on his warm, kind breast.

"The child's not been harmed?" asked Chiklin.

"I wouldn't dare," said Yelisey.

Nastya opened her eyes at Chiklin and wept for him. She thought that in the world everything existed truly and for always, and if Chiklin went away, she'd never find him anywhere on earth. In the barrack, Nastya often saw Chiklin in her dreams, and then she didn't want to fall asleep so that she wouldn't suffer in the morning, when it came without him.

Chiklin took the girl in his arms.

"You've been all right?"

"All right," said Nastya. "And you've made a kolkhoz here? Let me see the kolkhoz!"

Getting up from the ground, Chiklin pressed Nastya's head to his neck and went out to liquidate the kulaks.

"Zhachev didn't hurt you, did he?"

"Why would he hurt me, when I'll remain into socialism, and he will die soon."

"No, I guess he wouldn't hurt you," said Chiklin, and turned his attention to the crowds of people. Strangers, outsiders had come from somewhere and settled in clumps and masses all over the Orgyard, while the kolkhoz still slept together near last night's extinguished fire. In the kolkhoz street there were also people from other places. They stood silently in expectation of the joy for which Yelisey and the other kolkhoz messengers had brought them. Some of the strangers surrounded Yelisey and asked him:

"Well, where is the kolkhoz happiness—or did we come for nothing? How long are we to wander without a stop?"

"If we're brought here, the *activ* knows what for," answered Yelisey.

"That *activ* of yours, he must be sleeping?"

"The *activ* cannot sleep," said Yelisey.

The activist came out on the porch with his assistants, and next to him was Prushevsky. Zhachev crawled behind them all. Prushevsky was sent to the kolkhoz by Comrade Pashkin because Yelisey had passed by the foundation pit the previous day and ate gruel with Zhachev, but, lacking brains, he couldn't say a single word. When he heard about it, Pashkin decided to send Prushevsky full speed to the kolkhoz as a cadre of the cultural revolution, for organized people should not live without brains. As for Zhachev, he came of his own will, as a cripple. And that was why the three of them had come, with Nastya in their arms, not counting the roadside peasants who were told by Yelisey to follow him in order to rejoice in the kolkhoz.

"Go on and finish the raft, hurry up," Chiklin said to Prushevsky. "I'll come back to you soon."

Yelisey went with Chiklin to show him the most oppressed farm laborer, who had worked most of his life without pay for prosperous households, and now toiled as a hammerer in the kolkhoz smithy and received food as a blacksmith's helper. However, this hammerer was not a member of the kolkhoz but was considered a hired man, and the trade union line was deeply troubled when it received reports about this official hired laborer, the only one in the entire district. As for Pashkin, he was altogether upset about the unknown proletarian in the district and wanted to free him as quickly as possible from oppression.

Near the smithy stood a car and burned gasoline without moving from the spot. Pashkin, who had come there with his spouse, had just stepped out of it, to discover with avid zeal the last remaining hired farm laborer and, having provided him with a better lot in life, to dismiss the union's district committee for negligent service to the member masses. But before Chiklin and Yelisey got to the smithy, Comrade Pashkin had already left it and departed in his car with bowed head, as if he didn't know what to do next. Comrade Pashkin's spouse had not come out of the car at all: she was merely guarding the man she loved from chance women who adored her husband's power and took the firmness of his leadership as a token of the strength of love that he could give them.

Chiklin entered the smithy with Nastya in his arms, and Yelisey remained outside. The blacksmith was pumping air into the forge with his bellows, and a bear was striking a red-hot iron bar across the anvil with a hammer.

"Hurry, Mishka, we're a shock brigade, you know, you and I," the smith said.

But the bear was working so diligently even without any urging that the air smelled of burnt fur, singed by the flying sparks of metal, and he did not feel it.

"That will do, now!" decided the smith.

The bear stopped hammering and, stepping aside, drank half a pail of water to quench his thirst. Then, wiping his wearied proletarian face, the bear spat on his paw and went back to his job as hammerer. The smith had now set him to making a horseshoe for a certain individual peasant in the vicinity of the kolkhoz.

"Mish, we've got to make it quick: the customer is coming in the evening, we'll have a drink!" and the smith pointed to his throat as if it were a pipe for vodka. Understanding the future pleasure, the bear went to work on the horseshoe with even greater zeal.

"And what is it you wish, good man?" the smith asked Chiklin.

"Let the hammerer come and show us the kulaks: people say he's had lots of experience."

The smith considered it for a while, and said:

"Did you coordinate the problem with the *activ*? The smithy, you know, has an industrial-financial plan, and you're interfering with it."

"It's fully coordinated," answered Chiklin. "And if your plan falls back, I'll come to you myself to pull it up. . . . Have you heard about Mount Ararat? I'm sure I could raise it by myself if I kept piling earth on the same spot with my shovel."

"Well, take him, then," the smith said about the bear. "Go to the Orgyard and strike the bell, so Mishka would hear the lunch break, or he won't stir—he's a great one for discipline around here."

While Yelisey walked apathetically to the Orgyard, the bear made four horseshoes and begged for more labor. But the blacksmith sent him for firewood, to burn it later into coal, and the bear brought a whole suitable fence. Looking at the blackened, singed bear, Nastya rejoiced that he was for them, not for the bourgeois.

"He also suffers—so he's ours, isn't that so?" said Nastya.

"Naturally," answered Chiklin.

There was the booming of a bell, and the bear instantly abandoned his work without attention. Until then he was breaking up the fence into small pieces, but now he straightened up and sighed hopefully, as if to say, "That's it." He dipped his paws into a pail of water, to wash back cleanness on them, then he went outside to receive his food. The smith pointed at Chiklin, and the bear calmly followed the man, walking upright on his hind legs, as he was accustomed to. Nastya touched him on the shoulder, and he also touched her lightly with his paw and yawned with his whole mouth, blowing out the smell of past food.

"Look, Chiklin, he's all gray!"

"He lived with people, so he turned gray from sorrow."

The bear waited for the girl to look at him again, and when she did, he closed one eye and winked at her. Nastya laughed, and the hammerer struck himself on the belly, which made something gurgle there, and Nastya laughed still harder, but the bear paid no attention to the child.

Near some yards it was as cool as in the field, others gave off warmth. Cows and horses lay in the yards with open, putrefying bodies; the heat of life, accumulated over many years under the sun, was still rising from them into the air, into the general wintry space. Chiklin and the hammerer had already passed by many yards, but somehow they had not liquidated any kulaks anywhere.

The snow, which until then descended from upper places now and then, began to fall more densely and harshly; a wind strayed in and started to create a blizzard, which happens when winter is setting in. But Chiklin and the bear walked through the snowy, slashing mass straight down the street, because Chiklin could not consider nature's mood. He only hid Nastya from the cold inside his coat, leaving just her head outside, so she wouldn't get lonely in the warm darkness. The girl watched the bear all the time—she was glad that the animal was also the working class. And the hammerer looked at her as at a forgotten sister, with whom he fed at his mother's belly in the summer forest of his childhood. Wishing to gladden Nastya, the bear looked around—what could he seize and break off as a present to her? But there was no happy object to speak of nearby, nothing but clay and straw huts and wattle fences. Then the hammerer peered into the snowy wind, quickly caught in it something small and brought his closed paw to Nastya's face. Nastya took a fly out of his paw, though she knew that there were no flies around any more —they had died at the end of summer. The bear began to chase flies down the whole street—they flew in clouds, intermingled with the rushing snow.

"How come there are flies when it's winter?" asked Nastya.

"It's because of the kulaks, daughter," said Chiklin.

Nastya crushed in her hand the fat kulak fly the bear had given her and said:

"Kill them as a class! Or else there will be flies in winter, not in summer, and the birds will have nothing to eat."

The bear suddenly growled near a solidly built, clean hut and refused to go on, forgetting the fly and the girl. A woman's face stared out of the window, and the water of her tears flowed down the pane, as if she had been holding them in readiness all the time. The bear opened his maw at the visible woman and roared still more furiously, so that the woman jumped back inside the house.

"Kulaks!" said Chiklin and, entering the yard, opened the gates from inside. The bear also stepped across the property boundary into the yard.

Chiklin and the hammerer first examined the hiding places in the yard. In the barn, covered with chaff, lay three or more slaughtered sheep. When the bear touched one of the sheep with his foot, flies rose from it: they swarmed and battened in the hot meaty cracks of the bodies, and, diligently fed, flew with full bellies amid snow, never getting chilled in it.

A warmth came out of the barn—and in the cracks of the corpses it was probably as hot as in moldering turf in summertime, so that the flies lived there quite normally. Chiklin felt sick in the big barn; it seemed to him that bathhouse stoves were burning there, and Nastya closed her eyes from the stench and wondered why it was warm in the kolkhoz in the wintertime, without the four seasons of the year that Prushevsky had told her about at the foundation pit when birds stopped singing in the bare autumn fields.

The hammerer went from the barn to the house. In the

entrance hall he bellowed in a menacing voice and threw out across the porch a huge century-old trunk, from which spools of thread came flying.

In the house, Chiklin found only the woman and a boy; the boy sat puffing on a chamber pot, and his mother, crouching, nested in the middle of the room, as if all of her substance had dropped down below. She was no longer screaming, but merely opened her mouth and tried to breathe.

"Husband, husband!" she began to cry, unable to move in the feebleness of grief.

"What?" a voice came from atop the stove. Then a dried-out coffin creaked, and the master of the house climbed out.

"They've come," the woman said slowly. "Go meet them. . . . My bitter life!"

"Out!" Chiklin ordered the whole family.

The hammerer touched the boy's ear, and he jumped up from the pot. The bear, not knowing what it was, sat down himself to try out the low utensil.

The boy stood in his bare shirt and stared, wondering, at the sitting bear.

"Give me back the shitpot, Uncle!" he begged, but the hammerer growled at him, straining from the uncomfortable position.

"Out!" Chiklin said to the kulak population.

The bear let out a sound from his maw without moving from the pot, and the prosperous peasant answered:

"Don't yell, masters, we'll go ourselves."

The hammerer recalled how he used to pull out stumps in that peasant's fields and eat grass from silent hunger, because the man had fed him only in the evening—what was left over from the pigs, and the pigs would lie down in the troughs and eat up his portion in their sleep. Recalling this, the bear rose from the pot, embraced the peasant's body in the handiest way, and squeezed so hard that the fat and sweat came bursting out of him, while the bear roared into his head in a variety of voices; his anger, and all the human speech he heard had made him almost capable of speaking.

The prosperous peasant waited till the bear released him, then went out as he was into the street. He had already passed the window when the woman rushed after him, and the boy remained in the house without his parents. He stood a while in sad bafflement, snatched the pot from the floor, and ran with it after his mother and father.

"He's very sly," said Nastya about the boy who had taken his pot with him.

After that there were more kulaks. At the fourth yard the bear growled again, denoting the presence there of his class enemy. Chiklin gave Nastya to the hammerer and went into the hut by himself.

"What have you come for, dear man?" asked a friendly, calm peasant.

"Get out of here!" answered Chiklin.

"Why, have I displeased you?"

"We need a kolkhoz, don't undermine it!"

The peasant considered this unhurriedly, as though in the midst of a heart-to-heart talk.

"A kolkhoz isn't right for you. . . ."

"Get out, viper!"

"Well, you will turn the whole republic into a kolkhoz, and the whole republic will then be an individual property!"

Chiklin felt short of breath. He rushed to the door and opened it to make freedom visible. It was just so that he had once flung himself against the shut door of a prison, incapable of comprehending captivity, screaming out of the grinding strength of his heart. He turned away from the reasonable peasant to keep him from participating in his passing sorrow, which concerned only the working class.

"None of your business, rascal! We can appoint a Tsar when it's to our benefit, and we can overthrow him with a single breath. . . . And you—scram!"

At this point Chiklin seized the peasant across his body and carried him outside, where he threw him into the snow. The peasant's greed had kept him from marrying; he had spent all his flesh in accumulating property, in the happiness of a secure existence; and now he didn't know what to feel.

"Liquidated?" he said out of the snow. "Look out, today I'm gone, and tomorrow you'll be finished. And in the end, only your chief man will come into socialism!"

At the fifth yard the hammerer roared hatefully again. A shabby resident ran out of the house with a pancake in his hand. But the bear knew that this master used to beat him with the root of a tree whenever he would stop, too tired to keep on turning the millstone with the log attached to it. This wretched little peasant forced the bear to work his mill instead of the wind, to avoid paying taxes, while he himself was always whining that he was as poor as a hired laborer and eating with his woman under the blanket. When his wife got pregnant, the miller would make her an abortion with his own hands, loving only his grown son, whom he had long ago sent up to be a city Communist.

"Eat, Misha!" the peasant offered the pancake to the bear.

The bear wrapped the pancake around his paw and gave the peasant such a blow on the ear with this baked glove that his mouth creaked and he toppled over.

"Vacate the laborers' property!" said Chiklin to the prone man. "Get out of the kolkhoz and don't you dare to go on living in the world!"

The well-to-do peasant lay quietly a while, then came to.

"Show me a paper first that you're really somebody!"

"What kind of somebody am I?" said Chiklin. "I'm nobody. With us the only somebody's the party!"

"Then show me at least the party, I'd like to see it."

Chiklin said with a frugal smile:

"You'll never recognize it, I barely feel it myself. Report to the raft today, you scum of capitalism!"

"Let him ride the seas—here today, there tomorrow,

right?" said Nastya. "We wouldn't be happy with scum!"

Chiklin and the hammerer went on to liberate six more huts, built by the toiling flesh of hired laborers, and returned to the Orgyard, where the masses, purged of the kulak class, stood waiting for something.

Checking the kulak class, which had arrived in the yard, against the class stratification document, the activist found everything exactly right and rejoiced at the action of Chiklin and the smithy hammerer. Chiklin also approved of the activist.

"You're a conscious man, all right," he said. "You sniff out classes like an animal."

The bear could not express himself. He stood a while at the side, then went back to the smithy through the falling snow with the buzzing flies. Nastya alone looked after him and pitied the old, singed bear like a man.

Prushevsky had already finished the log raft and looked at everybody now with an air of readiness.

"You rotter," Zhachev said to him. "Why're you staring like a man apart? You need more courage. Crush friend and foe and save the dough! You think those are living men? Oh-ho! They're nothing but outside skin. We've a long way to go to find people, that's what I am sad for!"

At the activist's order, the kulaks bent down and began to push the raft straight toward the river valley. Zhachev crawled after the kulaks to make certain of their true departure downstream to the sea, and to reassure himself that socialism would come and Nastya would receive it as her dowry, while he, Zhachev, would perish sooner as a tired, outworn prejudice.

Having liquidated the kulaks into the distance, Zhachev did not calm down; in fact, for some unknown reason, he felt still worse. For a long time he watched the raft floating systematically down the delicate flowing river; he watched the evening wind ruffle the dark, dead water, streaming amid chilled meadows to its faraway abyss, and grief and desolation filled his heart. Because socialism didn't need the stratum of sad cripples, and he, too, would soon be liquidated into the distant silence.

The kulak class looked from the raft in one direction— at Zhachev. People wanted to mark forever their homeland and the last, happy man on it.

Now the kulak transport began to turn around the bend of the river, and Zhachev began to lose the visibility of the class enemy behind the shrubbery on the bank.

"Hey, parasites, good-bye!" Zhachev called down the river.

"Goo-d-bye!" replied the kulaks floating down to sea.

Forward-calling music struck up in the Orgyard. Zhachev hurriedly climbed up the steep clay bank to join the celebration of the kolkhoz, although he knew that only former participants of imperialism were rejoicing there, not counting Nastya and the other children.

The activist had set up a radio loudspeaker on the porch. A great campaign march came out of it, and the whole kolkhoz, together with the surrounding pedestrian guests, joyously shifted from foot to foot on the same spot. The kolkhoz peasants were radiant of face, as though freshly washed; now they regretted nothing; the unknown filled the cool emptiness of their spirits. When the music changed, Yelisey came out in the center, struck his sole upon the ground, and began to dance, never bending, or blinking his white eyes. He moved like a rod, alone among the standing peasants, his bones and body working in sharp rhythm. By and by, the peasants began to snort and circle around each other, and the women gaily raised their arms and started stamping their feet under their skirts. The guests threw down their sacks, called over the local girls, and sped along the ground at a brisk pace, kissing their partners as a special treat to themselves. The radio music excited life more and more; the passive peasants gave out shouts of pleasure, the more advanced ones did their best to develop the further tempos of the celebration in every way, and even the socialized horses, hearing the noise of human happiness, came one by one to the Orgyard and began to neigh.

The snowy wind died down; a misty moon appeared in the remote sky, emptied of storms and clouds—a sky that was so bare that it admitted eternal freedom, and so eerie that freedom needed friendship.

Under this sky, on the clean snow, already spotted here and there with flies, all the people rejoiced as comrades. Even those who had lived long on earth moved off their spots and shuffled, oblivious of themselves.

"Eh, you, Mother Esesar!"* a comical peasant shouted merrily, demonstrating his agility and slapping himself on the belly, the cheeks, and the mouth. "Hug her to your hearts, our motherland, she ain't married!"

"Is she a wench or a widow?" one of the nearby guests asked as he danced.

"A wench!" explained the dancing peasant. "Can't you see by all those fancy notions?"

"Let 'er play around a bit," the visiting guest agreed. "Let her have her fun! We'll tame her after a while—she'll be a quiet woman. Everything will be all right!"

Nastya slipped down from Chiklin's arms and also stamped her feet near the hell-bent peasants sweeping by, because that was what she wanted. Zhachev crawled among the dancers, tripping up those who were in his way, and gave the guest who wanted to marry off the young Esesar to a peasant a punch in the side, so he'd give up hoping.

"Don't you dare to think whatever comes into your head! Or are you looking for a trip downriver? We'll get you on the raft before you know it!"

The guest was now frightened that he had come at all.

"I won't think nothing any more, comrade cripple—I'll just whisper from now on."

*TRANSLATOR'S NOTE: SSR—Soviet Socialist Republic—a play on the old "Mother Russia." What follows is an oblique reference to the question of who would rule the country—the peasantry or the proletariat.

Chiklin looked for a long time at the jubilating mass of people and felt the peace of goodness in his breast. From the elevation of the porch he saw the moonlit purity of distant space, the sadness of the stilled snow, and the submissive sleep of the whole world, which had been built with so much effort and pain—forgotten now by everyone, so as to have no fear of living on.

"Nastya, don't get chilled too long, come here," called Chiklin.

"I'm not a bit cold—people breathe here," said Nastya, running away from Zhachev, who was roaring lovingly.

"Rub your hands, or you'll get numb: the air is big, and you are little!"

"I rubbed them already. Sit quiet!"

The radio stopped playing suddenly in the middle of a tune. But the people couldn't stop until the activist said, "Halt, till the next sound!"

Prushevsky managed to fix the radio quickly, but now there was no music, only a man's voice:

"Listen to our announcements: collect willow bark!"

And then the radio stopped again. Hearing the announcement, the activist thought hard for memory's sake, so he wouldn't forget about the willow bark campaign and get to be known throughout the district as a slacker, like last time, when he forgot to organize the shrub day, and now the whole kolkhoz was without twigs. Prushevsky went to work on the radio again, and time passed while the engineer diligently puttered with the mechanism with his chilled hands. But his efforts were unyielding, because he was not certain whether the radio would bring solace to the poor and a dear voice from somewhere to him.

Midnight must have been near; the moon stood high over the wattle fences and the meek, aged village, and the dead burdocks glistened, covered by tiny, frozen bits of snow. A stray fly tried to alight on an icy burdock, but immediately broke away and flew up, buzzing in the moonlit heights like a lark under the sun.

Without stopping its heavy, stomping dance, the kolkhoz gradually struck up a song in a weak voice. It was impossible to understand the words of this song, but one could hear in them the sorrowful happiness and the melody of a slowly wandering man.

"Zhachev!" said Chiklin. "Go and stop the movement. What is it—did they die of happiness? Dancing and dancing."

Zhachev crawled away with Nastya into the Orghouse and, settling her down to sleep, came out again.

"Hey, organized folk, quit dancing. Enough! Gone slap-happy, the scum!"

But the kolkhoz, carried away by the dance, paid no mind to his word and kept stomping heavily, covering itself with the song.

"Want to get it from me? Just wait a minute and you will!"

Zhachev crept down from the porch, entrenched himself in the midst of the busy feet, and began to grab people by their lower ends and tumble them on the ground for a rest. People dropped like empty trousers—Zhachev was sorry that they didn't seem to feel his hands—and instantly fell silent.

"Where can Voshchev be?" Chiklin worried. "What is he searching for in the distance, the petty proletarian?"

Tired of waiting for Voshchev, Chiklin went to look for him after midnight. He walked the length of the deserted village street, but no man was visible anywhere; only the bear snored in the smithy—the sound spread over the whole moonlit neighborhood—and the smith coughed from time to time.

It was quiet around, and beautiful. Chiklin stopped in the perplexity of thought. The bear still snored obediently, gathering strength for tomorrow's labor and a new feeling of life. He would no longer see the kulak class that used to torture him, and would rejoice in his existence. Now the hammerer would probably strike the horseshoes and the iron wheel-hoops with still more heartfelt diligence, since there was an unknown power in the world which left only those middle peasants in the village whom he liked, who were silently producing useful substance and felt partial happiness. As for the whole precise meaning of life and universal happiness, it had to languish in the breast of the proletarian happiness that was digging the ground, so that the hammerer's and Chiklin's hearts would merely hope and breathe, and their toiling hand be true and patient.

Chiklin carefully closed someone's wide-open gate, then examined the order of the street—whether everything was there. Seeing a peasant's coat being wasted on the road, he picked it up and brought it to the entranceway of the nearest hut: let it be saved for the good of the toilers.

Bending his body with trusting hope, Chiklin went along the backyards to look further for Voshchev. He climbed over fences, passed by the clay walls of huts, straightened leaning fenceposts, and constantly saw the bare endless winter that began just beyond the frail enclosures. Nastya could surely freeze in this alien world, because the earth was not for the easily chilled young. Only creatures like the hammerer could endure their life here, and even they turned gray from it.

"I wasn't even born yet, and you were already lying here, you poor unmoving thing!" the voice of Voshchev, of a man, said nearby. "That means, you've suffered a long time. Come and get warm!"

Chiklin turned his head sideways and noticed Voshchev bending down behind a tree and putting something into a sack, which was already full.

"What is it, Voshchev?"

"Oh, nothing," the other said, tying the neck of the sack and raising the load onto his shoulder.

The two of them went to the Orgyard to spend the night. The moon was now much lower, the village cast black shadows; everything was silent, and only the river, congealed by cold, was stirring between its familiar village banks.

The kolkhoz slept immovably in the Orgyard. Inside the Orghouse burned the light of safety—a single lamp for the entire extinguished village. By the lamp sat the activist at his mental labor: he was drawing graphs for the record in which he wished to enter all the data concerning the welfare of the poor and middle peasantry, so there would be a permanent, formal picture and experience, as a basis.

"Write down my goods, too!" said Voshchev, unpacking his sack.

He had gathered in the village all the poor, rejected objects, all the small unknown and forgotten things—to be avenged by socialism. Those patient, shabby rags had once touched the flesh of the laborers, and these things were marked forever by the burden of bowed life, expended without conscious meaning and lost without glory somewhere under the straw of the earth. Without full understanding, Voshchev had collected like a miser a sackful of material remnants of lost people, who had lived like him without truth and who had died before the victorious conclusion. Now he was presenting those liquidated toilers before the face of the government and the future, so that those who lay quietly in the depths of the earth could be avenged through the organization of the eternal meaning of man.

The activist began to make a record of the things that Voshchev brought in a special column he organized at the side, under the title of "List of Kulaks Liquidated to Death as a Class by the Proletariat, as Per Extinct Property Remnants." Instead of people, the activist entered evidences of existence: a bast shoe from the last century, a leaden earring from a shepherd's ear, a trouserleg of homespun cloth, and a variety of other equipment of a laboring but propertyless body.

By then Zhachev, who slept next to Nastya on the floor, managed accidentally to wake her.

"Turn away your mouth. You don't clean your teeth, you fool," said Nastya to the cripple who shielded her against the cold draft from the door. "The bourgeois cut off your legs, and now you want your teeth to fall out too?"

Frightened, Zhachev closed his mouth and began to blow the air through his nose. The girl stretched, fixed the warm headkerchief in which she slept, but could not fall asleep again because she was too wide-awake.

"Did they bring rags for reuse?" she asked about Voshchev's sack.

"No," said Chiklin. "It's toys for you—get up and choose what you want."

Nastya rose to her height, stamped a bit for developing her body, then, lowering herself on the spot, grasped the registered pile of objects between her legs. Chiklin brought the lamp down for her from the table, so that the girl could better see what she liked—the activist could write without mistakes in the dark as well.

After a while, the activist slipped the record down to the floor, so the child would sign that she received in full the entire accumulated property of kinless dead laborers and would use it in time to come. Nastya slowly drew a hammer and sickle on the paper and returned the document.

Chiklin took off his quilted cotton jacket and his shoes, and walked about the floor in socks, peaceful and pleased that there was no one now to rob Nastya of her share of living in the world, that rivers flowed only into the depths of seas, and that those who had floated away in the raft would not return to torture the hammerer—Mikhail. As for the nameless people of whom nothing was left but bast shoes and earrings, they did not need to pine forever in the earth, but neither could they rise.

"Prushevsky," said Chiklin.

"Yes," answered the engineer; he was sitting in the cor-

ner, leaning against it with his back, and dozed indifferently. His sister had not written him for a long time. If she
was dead, he decided to go and cook food for her children,
to weary himself out till he lost his soul and ended some day
as an old man, accustomed to live without feeling; this was
the same as dying now, but sadder yet; if he went, he could
live in his sister's place, and remember longer and with
greater sorrow the young woman who had passed by him
in his youth, now probably not likely any more to be alive.
Prushevsky wanted to keep her in the world a little longer,
even if only in his secret feeling—that agitated young
woman, forgotten by everyone if she was dead, cooking
soup for her children if alive.

"Prushevsky! Will the achievements of higher science be
able to restore rotted people back to life, or won't they?"

"They won't," said Prushevsky.

"You're lying," Zhachev said reproachfully, without
opening his eyes. "Marxism will be able to do anything. Or
why is Lenin lying whole in Moscow? He's waiting for
science—he wants to be revived. I'd find work for Lenin
too," he added. "I'd show him who else should get a thing
or two in addition! Somehow, I can spot vermin at first
glance!"

"You're a fool, that's what," Nastya explained as she
rummaged in the laborers' rags. "You only see, but one
must work. Right, Uncle Voshchev?"

Voshchev had already covered himself with the empty
sack and lay listening to the beating of his witless heart,
which drew his entire body into some undesirable distance
of life.

"Who knows," he answered Nastya. "You work and
work, and when you come to the end, when you learn
everything, you get tired and die. Don't grow up, child—
it will make you sad."

Nastya was displeased.

"Only kulaks should die, and you're a fool. Zhachev,
watch over me, I want to sleep again."

"Come, girl," said Zhachev. "Come to me from that kulak spawn. He wants to get it—tomorrow he will!"

Everyone was silent, patiently continuing the night. Only the activist wrote unceasingly, and achievements kept expanding before his conscious mind, so that he fretted about himself: "You're doing harm to the Union, you passive devil. You could have sent the whole district into collectivization, and here you're fussing with a single kolkhoz. It's time to send the population into socialism by the trainload, and you stick all the time to narrow perspectives. Eh, trouble!"

Somebody's quiet hand tapped on the door out of the pure moonlit silence, and in the sound of that hand one could still hear remnants of timidity.

"Come in, we aren't having a meeting," said the activist.

"Oh, well," the man replied from outside, not entering. "I thought—maybe you're thinking."

"Come in, don't irritate me," said Zhachev.

Yelisey entered. He had already slept his fill on the ground; his eyes darkened with inner blood, and he had grown stronger from the habit of being organized.

"The bear is banging in the smithy and growling a song. The whole kolkhoz was awakened, we got scared without you."

"We must go and see what's up," the activist decided.

"I'll go myself," said Chiklin. "You sit and write: your business is to keep accounts."

"That's only while there are fools!" Zhachev warned the activist. "Soon we will activate everybody; just let the masses reach the limit of their troubles, let the children grow up!"

Chiklin went to the smithy. The night spread vast and cool over him, stars shone generously over the snowy purity of the earth, and the hammerer's strokes spread wide, as though the bear became ashamed of sleeping under these expectant stars and answered them in the one way he could. The bear's a proper proletarian old man, Chiklin thought with respect. The bear gave out a long, contented growl, announcing aloud a happy song.

The smithy was open to the moonlit night, to the whole bright surface of the earth; a fire burned in the forge, kept going by the smith himself, who lay stretched out on the ground and rhythmically pulled the bellows rope. And the hammerer, completely pleased, was forging wheel-hoops and singing a song.

"Won't let me sleep," the smith complained. "Got up and started roaring. I lit the forge for him, and he went on a working binge. . . . He's always quiet, and suddenly he's like a crazy one!"

"Why's that?" asked Chiklin.

"Who knows! Yesterday he came back from the liquidation of the kulaks and kept shuffling and growling something in a cheery way. I guess it pleased him. And then one of the activist's helpers passed by—he brought a piece of cloth and strung it up along the fence. Mishka kept looking over at it and figuring something out. As if to say: the kulaks are gone, and that's why the red slogan is hung there. I could see something coming into his head and staying there. . . ."

"All right, you go to sleep, I'll tend the fire," said Chiklin. He took the rope and began to pump air into the forge, so the hammerer could make wheel irons for kolkhoz use.

Toward morning dawn, yesterday's visiting peasants began to disperse through the vicinity. But the kolkhoz had nowhere to go, and, getting up from the Orgyard, they started out toward the smithy, from which came the sounds of the hammerer's work. Prushevsky and Voshchev went with the rest and watched Chiklin helping the bear. Near the smithy an exclamation hung on the fence, painted on a flag: "For the party, for loyal devotion to it, for shock work, pushing open for the proletariat the door to the future!"

When he tired, the hammerer went outside and ate snow

to cool himself off, and then again the hammer leaped into iron pulp, constantly increasing the speed of the strokes. The hammerer had now stopped singing altogether. He expended his whole furious silent joy in the zeal of labor, and the kolkhoz peasants gradually sympathized with him and collectively grunted in time to the sledgehammer blows, so as to make the hoops stronger and safer. After watching a while, Yelisey advised the hammerer:

"Go slower, Mish, then the hoop won't be brittle and won't snap. And you're battering the iron as if it's some son of a bitch. The iron's also property, it's no good treating it this way!"

But the bear opened his maw at Yelisey, and Yelisey moved off, worrying about the iron. However, the other peasants couldn't bear the spoilage any more, either.

"Don't hit so hard, you devil!" they buzzed. "Don't damage what belongs to all: property's just like an orphan now, there's no one to feel sorry for it. . . . Slower, slower, you goblin!"

"Stop bashing the iron! What d'you think, it's private, eh?"

"Get out, cool off, you devil! Get tired, you wooly idol!"

"He ought to be kicked out of the kolkhoz, that's what. Why should we take losses? Did you ever!"

But Chiklin pumped air into the forge, and the hammerer tried to keep up with the fire and crushed the iron as if it was the enemy of life; if there were no kulaks, then there was no one but the bear in the world.

"Trouble!" sighed the kolkhoz members.

"A fine thing—everything will bust now! The iron will be full of holes!"

"A punishment from on high. . . . And you can't touch him either—they'll say, a propertyless fellow, they'll talk of proletariat, industrialization. . . ."

"'That's nothing. Now, if they talk of losing a cadre, then we'll be in a bad way."

"Cadre, nothing. Now, if the instructor comes, or Comrade Pashkin himself, they'll make it hot for us!"

"And what if nothing happens? What if we let him have it, eh?"

"You crazy, or what? He's a union man. Comrade Pashkin came down specially the other day—it's not so jolly for him either without laborers."

Yelisey spoke less than anyone, but worried almost more than anybody else. When he had his own household, he didn't sleep nights—kept an eye on everything, lest something go wrong, lest a horse overeat or overdrink, lest a cow get into a mood. And now, when the whole kolkhoz, the whole world hereabouts was placed in his care—because he felt the others were not to be relied on—his stomach ached in advance out of anxiety for all that property.

"We'll sicken, all of us!" said a middle peasant who had lived silently through the entire revolution. "Before, I had to worry about my family, and now you've got to think about everybody—it'll be the death of us altogether, for such measly keep."

Voshchev felt sad that a beast was laboring so hard, as if he sensed life's meaning nearby, while he stood still and wasn't breaking into the door of the future: maybe there was something out there, after all. By this time Chiklin finished pumping air and joined the bear in making spikes for a harrow. Oblivious of the watching people and the entire outlook, the two workmen tirelessly labored as their conscience dictated, which was as it should be. The hammerer forged the spikes, and Chiklin tempered them, though he didn't know exactly how long they should be held in water to obtain the proper hardness.

"And what if a spike hits a rock?" Yelisey groaned. "If it hits anything hard, it'll split in half!"

"Take the iron out of the water, you devil!" cried the kolkhoz. "Stop torturing the material!"

Chiklin took out the oversoaked metal, when Yelisey came into the smithy, took the pliers from him, and began to temper the spikes with his own two hands. Other organized peasants also rushed inside the establishment and, with eased souls, began to toil over the iron objects with that careful zeal that comes when benefit is more essential than damage. I must remember to whitewash the smithy, Yelisey thought calmly as he worked. It's all sooty—what kind of efficiency is that?

"Now tug at the rope," said Yelisey. "But not too fast—rope's expensive nowadays, and new bellows are way over the kolkhoz treasury!"

"I'll do it quictly," said Voshchev, and began to tug and slacken the rope, forgetting himself in the patience of labor.

The morning of a winter day was rising, and the usual light spread over the district. But the lamp still burned in the Orgyard, until Yelisey noticed this superfluous fire. Having noticed it, he went there and put out the lamp, to save kerosene.

The young girls and the adolescents, who had slept in the huts, were up now. In general, they were indifferent to the anxiety of their fathers; they were not interested in their anguish and they endured the poverty at home without attention, living at the expense of their feeling of still unresponsive happiness, which had to happen anyway. Most of the young girls and the growing generation went to the reading-room hut in the morning and remained there without eating all day, learning reading and writing and numbers, getting used to friendship, and imagining things in anticipation. When the kolkhoz seized upon the smithy, Prushevsky alone remained at the side, standing without motion by the fence. He did not know why he had been sent to this village or how to live forgotten among the masses, and he decided to appoint precisely the day of the end of his presence on earth. Taking out his notebook, he entered in it a late evening hour of a day in the dead of winter: let everybody settle down to sleep; the frozen earth will grow silent of the noises of all construction, and he, wherever he might be, will lie down with his face up and cease breathing. For no edifice, no satisfaction, no dear friend, nor the conquest of stars can overcome the impoverishment of his spirit; no matter what, he will feel the futility of friendship based neither on excellence, nor on physical love, and endure the boredom of the most remote stars, whose depths hold the same copper ores, and where the same Supreme National Economic Soviet will be needed.

It seemed to Prushevsky that all his emotions, all his desires and his old longings met in his reasoning mind and gained awareness of themselves down to the very sources of their origin, mortally destroying the naïveté of hope. But the origin of emotions remained a troubling place in life; by dying, one could lose forever this single happy, true area of existence without having entered it. But good God, what was to be done if he lacked any of those self-oblivious impressions that quicken life and make it rise and stretch its arms forward toward hope?

Prushevsky covered his face with his hands. Let reason be the synthesis of all emotions where all the currents of anxious movement are stilled and pacified; but where did the anxiety and the movement come from? He did not know, all he knew was that reason's old age was the longing for death, his only feeling. And then, perhaps, he would close the circle—return to the origin of feelings, to the summer evening of his never-repeated meeting.

"Comrade! Are you the one who's come to us for cultural revolution?"

Prushevsky dropped his hands from his eyes. Nearby, young women and adolescents walked to the reading-room hut. One girl stood before him—in felt boots and a worn shawl on her trusting head. Her eyes looked at the engineer with wondering love, because she could not grasp the power of knowledge hidden in this man. She would have agreed to love him, a gray-haired stranger, forever and with devotion; she would have agreed to bear his children, to torment her body daily, if only he would teach her to know the whole world and take part in it. Nothing meant anything to her—her youth, her happiness; she sensed nearby a rushing, ardent movement, her heart rose up in the wind of the general striving life, but she could not utter the words of her joy, and now she stood and begged him to teach her those words, that ability to feel the whole world's light within one's head, and help it glow. The girl did not yet know whether the learned man would come with her, and looked at him, uncertain, ready to study again with the activist.

"I'll come with you in a moment," said Prushevsky.

The girl wanted to cry out with joy, but she did not, for fear that he might be offended.

"Come," said Prushevsky.

The girl walked ahead, pointing the way to the engineer, although it would have been impossible to go wrong; but she wanted to express her gratitude, and had no gift for the man who followed her.

The kolkhoz members burnt up all the coal in the smithy, used up the whole stock of iron for useful articles, mended all dead inventory, and, sorrowing over the end of their labor, left the establishment, worried that the kolkhoz might now go downhill. The hammerer tired himself out before them; he climbed out a bit earlier to eat some snow and quench his thirst, and as the snow was thawing in his mouth the bear dozed off and toppled over with his whole body, to rest.

Outside, the kolkhoz sat down by the fence and sat there, looking over at the village, while the snow melted under the motionless peasants. Having stopped work, Voshchev again fell into thought, without moving from the spot.

"Wake up!" Chiklin said to him. "Lie down with the bear and forget everything."

"The truth, Comrade Chiklin, can't be forgotten. . . ."

Chiklin seized Voshchev across his body and laid him down next to the sleeping bear.

"Lie quiet," he said, standing over him. "The bear

breathes, and you can't! The proletariat endures, and you're afraid! Ugh, you vermin!"

Voshchev huddled close to the hammerer, got warm, and fell asleep.

A rider from the district leaped into the street on a quivering horse.

"Where's the *activ?*" he shouted to the sitting kolkhoz, without losing speed.

"Gallop straight ahead!" the kolkhoz informed him. "But don't turn either right or left!"

"I won't!" cried the rider, already from afar, and only the pouch with the directives bumped against his thigh.

A few minutes later the same rider galloped back, waving the receipt book in the air so that the wind would dry the ink of the activist's signature. The well-fed horse churned up the snow, exposing the soil as he flew by, then disappeared in the distance.

"What a horse he's ruining, the bureaucrat!" thought the kolkhoz. "Enough to make you sick."

Chiklin took an iron rod in the smithy and brought it to the child as a toy. He liked to bring her various objects in silence, so that the girl would understand without words his joy for her.

Zhachev had long been up. But Nastya, her tired lips slightly open, continued sadly and involuntarily to sleep.

Chiklin carefully looked at the child—whether she hadn't been hurt in any way since yesterday, whether her body was completely sound. But the child was quite in order, except that her face was burning from inner childish strength. The activist's tear dropped on the directive— Chiklin noticed it at once. The active leader sat motionless at the table, just as he had sat last night. It had been with a sense of satisfaction that he dispatched, with the district rider, the completed report on the liquidation of the class enemy and all the achievements of local activity. But now a new directive had descended on him, signed for some reason by the province center, over the heads of the district and the region, and the directive that lay before him noted the undesirable phenomena of overdoing, overreaching, excessive zeal, and all kinds of slippage down the right and the left slope from the clear-cut ridge of the proper party line. Besides, the *activ* was ordered to manifest prominent vigilance in the direction of the middle peasants; since they had rushed into the kolkhozes, couldn't this general fact be a mysterious plot instigated by the kulak masses, as if to say: let's join the kolkhozes with our entire future flood and wash away the shores of the leadership; then there won't be enough government for us—we'll tire it out.

"According to the latest materials in the hands of the province committee," the directive concluded, "we can see, for example, that the *activ* of the General Line Kolkhoz had already strayed into the leftist mire of rightist opportunism. The organizer of the local kolkhoz asks the above-placed organization whether there is anything beyond the kolkhoz and the commune that is higher and brighter, in order to move in that direction the poor and middle masses which are irresistibly straining toward the vistas of future history, toward the highest peak of unseen universal times. This comrade asks us to send him model regulations for such an organization, as well as blanks, a penholder and pens, and two pints of ink. He does not understand to what extent he is here speculating on the sincere and basically healthy feeling of the middle peasant, which brings him into the kolkhoz. It is impossible not to admit that such a comrade is a wrecker of the party, an objective enemy of the proletariat, and must be removed from leadership immediately and forever."

The activist's weakened heart skipped a beat, and he wept tears on the paper from the province.

"What's the matter, you bastard?" Zhachev asked him.

But the activist did not answer. Had he seen any joy in recent times, had he eaten or slept his fill, or loved even one poor peasant girl? He felt himself as in delirium, his heart was scarcely beating with the strain of his duties, he tried to organize happiness only outside of himself, and earn, at least in perspective, a post at the district.

"Answer me, parasite, or you'll get it in a minute!" Zhachev spoke again. "I'll bet you've been wrecking our republic, you vermin!"

Pulling down the directive from the table, Zhachev began personally to study it on the floor.

"I want my mama!" said Nastya, waking up.

Chiklin bent down to the saddened child.

"Mama is dead, girl. I am left now!"

"Why do you carry me around, where are the four seasons of the year? See what terrible heat I have under my skin! Take off my shirt, it'll burn up and I'll have nothing to wear when I get well."

Chiklin touched Nastya. She was hot and damp, her bones stuck out pitifully from within. How tender and peaceful the surrounding world had to be, so she would be alive!

"Cover me, I want to sleep. I won't remember anything, or it will be too sad to be sick, won't it?"

Chiklin removed his entire outer clothing; he also took the activist's and Zhachev's quilted jackets, and wrapped Nastya in all those warm things. She closed her eyes and felt good in the warmth and in sleep, as if she were flying amid cool air. In the course of passing time, Nastya had grown a little and looked more and more like her mother.

"I knew it, I knew he was a rat," Zhachev pronounced judgment on the activist. "Well, what will you do with this member now?"

"Why, what does it say?"

"They write things that you must agree with them!"

"Try not to agree," said the active man with tears in his eyes.

"Eh, what trouble with the revolution." Zhachev became seriously upset. "Where is she, then, the out-and-out scurvy thing? Come here, you bitch, and get it from a crippled soldier!"

Feeling his thought in loneliness, and not wishing to expend his substance thanklessly on the government and the future generation, the activist took his jacket back from Nastya. If he was being removed, let the masses warm their own selves. And he stopped with the jacket in his hands in the middle of the Orghouse—without any further desire to live, with big tears rolling down, and in doubt of spirit that capitalism might still, perhaps, appear.

"Why'd you uncover the child?" asked Chiklin. "Want to chill her?"

"Nuts to your child!" said the activist.

Zhachev glanced at Chiklin and advised him:

"Get the iron you brought from the smithy!"

"What are you saying!" answered Chiklin. "I've never in my life touched any man with a dead weapon; how would I feel justice if I did?"

Then Chiklin calmly gave the activist a hand blow in the chest, so that children could still have hope instead of freezing. A feeble crunch of bones came from inside the activist, and the whole man toppled on the floor. Chiklin looked at him with satisfaction, like a man who had just done a necessary, useful thing. The activist's jacket dropped from his hands and lay separately, covering no one.

"Cover him," Chiklin said to Zhachev. "Let him get warm."

Zhachev immediately dressed the activist in his jacket and at the same time felt the man, to see how whole he was.

"Is he alive?" asked Chiklin.

"So-so—in between," Zhachev answered joyfully. "But all the same, Comrade Chiklin, your hand works like a sledgehammer—you had nothing to do with it."

"Well, why does he undress a fevered child!" Chiklin said angrily. "He could have made some tea to warm himself."

A blizzard arose in the village, although no storm could be heard. Zhachev opened the window to check and saw that it was the kolkhoz sweeping up the snow for hygiene's sake; the peasants now did not like to see the snow spotted by the flies, they wanted a cleaner winter.

Finishing the job in the Orgyard, the kolkhoz members did not go on with the work and dropped under the shed, puzzled about their further life. Although the people had not eaten for a long time, they were not drawn to food even now, because their stomachs were still overloaded with the abundance of meat they had consumed in the recent past. Taking advantage of the peaceful sadness of the kolkhoz and the invisibility of the *activ*, the old man from the tile factory and other dubious elements who had until then been imprisoned in the Orgyard came out of the back pantries and various concealed obstacles to life, and set off into the distance on their own daily business.

Chiklin and Zhachev leaned over Nastya from both sides, the better to guard her. From her inescapable heat the girl became dark and submissive, and only her brain thought sorrowfully:

"I want to be with mama again," she said without opening her eyes.

"Your mama isn't living any more," Zhachev said joylessly. "Everybody dies from life—only the bones are left."

"I want her bones," begged the girl. "Who is that crying in the kolkhoz?"

Chiklin listened carefully. But everything was quiet around—nobody was crying, there was no reason to cry. The day had already reached its middle, the pale sun stood high over the land, some distant masses moved along the horizon to an unknown intervillage meeting—nothing could make any noise. Chiklin went out on the porch. A low, unconscious moan floated across the silent kolkhoz, then repeated itself. The sound began somewhere at the side, returning to an unpeopled place, and was not meant to be a complaint.

"Who is that?" shouted Chiklin from the height of the porch across the entire village, so that the dissatisfied one would hear him.

"It's the hammerer whining," answered the kolkhoz, lying under the shed. "At night he growled songs."

Indeed, except for the bear, there was nobody to cry now. He must have dug his snout into the earth, and howled sadly into the thick of the soil without understanding his grief.

"The bear out there's unhappy about something," Chiklin said to Nastya, returning to the room.

"Call him to me, I'm unhappy too," begged Nastya. "Take me to mama, it's very hot here!"

"In a minute, Nastya. Zhachev, crawl out for the bear. He has nothing to do, anyway—there's no material."

But Zhachev was barely gone when he returned: the bear was coming himself to the Orgyard, together with Voshchev, who held him by the paw as though he were weak, while the hammerer moved next to him at a sad pace.

Entering the Orghouse, the hammerer sniffed the lying activist and stood himself indifferently in the corner.

"I brought him as a witness that there is no truth," said Voshchev. "He can only work, you know, but as soon as he rests a while he starts feeling miserable. Let him exist now like a thing—to be remembered forever—I'll treat everybody!"

"Treat the coming swine," Zhachev agreed. "Preserve the wretched product for them!"

Voshchev bent down and began to gather the shabby things taken out by Nastya into his sack, for future revenge. Chiklin picked up Nastya in his arms, and she opened her sunken, silenced eyes, dried out like leaves. Through the window the girl stared at the kolkhoz peasants huddled close to one another, lying under the shed in patient forgetfulness.

"Voshchev, will you take the bear away with the rags for reuse too?" Nastya asked with concern.

"Naturally. I guard even decayed, dead things, and that's a poor living creature!"

"And what about them?" Nastya stretched her sick hand, thin as a lamb's foot, toward the kolkhoz lying in the yard.

133

Voshchev threw a proprietary glance at the yard and turned away, bowing his truth-hungry head even lower.

The activist was still silent on the floor, until the pensive Voshchev bent over him and shook him, out of a sense of curiosity before every damage to life. But the activist, dead or pretending, made no response. Then Voshchev squatted down near the man and for a long time looked into his blind, open face, withdrawn into the depths of its sorrowful consciousness.

The bear was silent a while, then started whimpering again, and his voice brought the whole kolkhoz from the Orgyard into the house.

"Well, Comrade *activ*, how are we to live now?" the kolkhoz asked. "You'd better worry about us, because we can't endure! Our inventory's now in order, the seed is clean, it's wintertime—there's nothing we can feel in it. See what you can do, try!"

"There's nobody to worry," said Chiklin. "There's your chief worrier, lying there."

The kolkhoz calmly stared at the prone activist, without pity, but without joy either, because the activist had always spoken precisely and correctly, strictly according to the rules, but he himself was so disgusting that when the community had once decided to marry him off in order to reduce his activity, even the homeliest women and girls burst out crying with misery.

"He's dead," Voshchev announced to everybody, getting up from the floor. "He knew everything, but he came to an end too."

"Maybe he's still breathing?" Zhachev wondered. "Try and see, please. Or else, he hasn't gotten it from me yet, and I will add my own share in a minute!"

Voshchev leaned again over the body of the activist, who had once done everything with such brutal importance, as if the whole world's truth, the whole meaning of life were inside him and nowhere else, while nothing was left to Voshchev except torment of the mind, lack of consciousness in the rushing current of existence, and the docility of a blind element.

"You rotter!" Voshchev whispered over the silent body. "So that is why I didn't know any meaning! You must have sucked it up not only out of me, but out of the whole class, you dry soul, and we are wandering like a quiet, dense mass and know nothing!"

And Voshchev struck the activist on the forehead—to enforce his death, and for his own conscious happiness.

Sensing his full mind, though still unable to speak or put its primal strength to action, Voshchev rose to his feet and said to the kolkhoz:

"I'll worry about you now!"

"Do!" the kolkhoz spoke unanimously.

Voshchev opened the door of the Orghouse into space and felt the desire to live into that unfenced distance, where the heart could beat, not only from cold air, but also from the true joy of mastering the whole dim substance of the earth.

"Take out the dead body!" Voshchev ordered.

"Where to?" asked the kolkhoz. "He can't be buried without music nohow. Put on the radio at least!"

"Liquidate him like a kulak down the river into the sea!" Zhachev had an idea.

"Can be done!" the kolkhoz agreed. "The water is still flowing."

Several men lifted the activist's body high and carried it to the river bank. Chiklin kept Nastya in his arms all the time, prepared to go with her to the foundation pit, but was delayed by the events that were transpiring.

"The juice is coming out of me everywhere," said Nastya. "Hurry up, you elderly fool, take me to mama! I feel bad!"

"We'll go right away, girl. I'll run over there with you. Yelisey, go call Prushevsky, tell him we're leaving. Voshchev will stay here for everybody, the child has taken sick."

Yelisey went and returned alone. Prushevsky didn't

want to come, he said he must first finish teaching the young here, or they might perish in the future, and he pitied them.

"Well, let him stay," Chiklin agreed. "So long as he's all right himself."

Zhachev, being a cripple, could not walk fast, but only crawled. Therefore Chiklin arranged for Yelisey to carry Nastya, while he carried Zhachev. And so, hurrying, they walked to the foundation pit along the wintry road.

"Look after Mishka the bear!" Nastya cried, turning around. "I'll come and visit him soon."

"Don't worry, young lady," the kolkhoz promised.

By evening the pedestrians caught sight of the city's electric lights in the distance. Zhachev had long tired of sitting in Chiklin's arms and said they ought to have taken a horse in the kolkhoz.

"We'll get there faster on foot," answered Yelisey. "Our horses have forgotten how to ride—standing all that time! They've even got swollen feet; all the walking they do is to steal some fodder."

When the travelers reached their place, they saw that the whole foundation pit was filled with snow, and the barrack was dark and empty. Chiklin put Zhachev down and began to go about making a fire to get Nastya warm, but she said:

"Bring me mama's bones, I want them!"

Chiklin sat down opposite the girl, all the time building a fire for light and warmth, and sent Zhachev to find milk somewhere. Yelisey sat for a long time on the threshold of the barrack, watching the bright nearby city where something made a constant noise and was regularly agitated in the general unrest. Then he rolled over on his side and fell asleep without eating.

People walked past the barrack, but nobody came in to see the sickened Nastya because everybody bowed his head and thought unceasingly about total collectivization.

Sometimes a silence fell suddenly, and then again train whistles sang in the distance, pile drivers let out steam, and voices of shock brigades rose in shouts as they hoisted something heavy—social benefits were being pushed continually forward all around.

"Chiklin, why do I always feel my mind and can never forget it?" wondered Nastya.

"I don't know, child. Probably because you've never seen anything good."

"And why do they work at night in the city instead of sleeping?"

"That's because they are concerned about you."

"And I am lying here all sick. . . . Chiklin, put mama's bones next to me, I'll put my arms around them and go to sleep. I'm so lonely now."

"Sleep, maybe you'll forget your mind."

The weakened Nastya suddenly raised herself and kissed Chiklin, who was bending over her, on his mustache. Like her mother, she knew how to kiss people first, without warning.

Chiklin was numb with the repeated happiness of his life and breathed silently over the child, until he got worried again about that little, fevered body.

To protect Nastya from the wind and to warm her generally, Chiklin lifted Yelisey from the threshold and laid him by the child's side.

"Lie here," Chiklin said to Yelisey, who was frightened in his sleep. "Put your arm around the girl and breathe on her often."

Yelisey did as he told him, and Chiklin lay down at the side, on his elbow, keenly listening with his drowsy head to the restless noise of the city construction works.

By midnight Zhachev appeared; he brought a bottle of cream and two pastries. He couldn't find anything else, since the new officials were not in their homes but were having a good time somewhere else. All tired out, Zhachev finally decided to fine Comrade Pashkin, as his most reliable resource; but Pashkin wasn't home either—he turned out to have gone to the theater with his wife. Therefore

Zhachev had to make his appearance at the show, amid the darkness and attention to some suffering elements on the stage, and loudly call Pashkin to the buffet, stopping the action of the art. Pashkin came out instantly, bought products for Zhachev in the buffet without a word, and hurriedly returned to the performance hall, to go on worrying there.

"I'll have to go to Pashkin again tomorrow," said Zhachev, quieting down in the distant corner of the barrack. "Let him put a stove here, or this wooden wagon will never get us to socialism!"

Chiklin wakened early in the morning; he was chilled, and he listened to Nastya. It was quiet and barely turning light, and only Zhachev growled his anxiety in his sleep.

"Are you breathing there, you middling devil?" Chiklin asked Yelisey.

"I'm breathing, Comrade Chiklin, sure I am. I've been blowing warmth on the child all night!"

"Well?"

"The girl isn't breathing, Comrade Chiklin—she's grown cold somehow."

Chiklin slowly rose from the ground and stopped. After standing a while, he went to where Zhachev was lying, to see if the cripple had not demolished the cream and the pastries. Then he found a broom and cleared the whole barrack of the diverse accumulated litter that had been blown there while it stood empty.

Putting the broom in its place, Chiklin felt a desire to dig the ground. He broke the lock of the forgotten storeroom with the spare inventory, pulled out a spade, and went unhurriedly to the foundation pit. He began to dig, but the soil was already frozen, and Chiklin had to hack the earth into lumps and pry it out in whole dead pieces. Deeper down it was softer and warmer. Chiklin plunged in with chopping blows of the iron spade and soon disappeared in the silent depth to nearly his full height. But even there he couldn't weary himself out, and began to shatter the ground sideways, breaking open the earth's closeness into width. The spade struck a slab of native rock and bent from the force of the blow. Then Chiklin flung it out with its handle onto the daytime surface and leaned his head against the bared clay.

In all these actions he tried to forget his mind now, but his mind never moved off the thought that Nastya was dead.

"I'll go and get another spade," said Chiklin and climbed out of the pit.

In the barrack, in order not to believe his mind, he went up to Nastya and felt her head; then he put his hand on Yelisey's forehead, checking his life by the warmth.

"Why is she cold, and you're hot?" asked Chiklin and didn't hear the answer, because now his mind forgot itself without his help.

After that Chiklin sat all the time on the earth floor, and the awakened Zhachev was with him, holding motionless in his hands the bottle of cream and the two pastries. And Yelisey, who had been breathing on the girl all night without sleeping, got tired now and fell asleep next to her, and slept until he heard the neighing voices of his familiar socialized horses.

Voshchev entered the barrack, followed by Mishka the bear and the entire kolkhoz, but the horses remained waiting outside.

"What's the matter?" Zhachev said seeing Voshchev. "Why did you leave the kolkhoz—do you want our whole earth to die? Or are you hankering to get it from the proletariat? Come over here, then—you'll get what's coming to you from me as a class!"

But Voshchev had already gone out to the horse without hearing out Zhachev. He had brought a present for Nastya —a whole bag of specially selected trash in the form of rare toys that weren't for sale, every one of which was an eternal memory of a forgotten human being. But Nastya, though she looked at Voshchev, showed no joy, and Voshchev touched her, seeing her open, silenced mouth and her indifferent, weary body. Voshchev stood puzzled over the stilled child. He no longer knew where communism would now be on earth if it didn't exist first in a child's feeling and convinced impression. What need had he now of the meaning of life and the truth of universal origin, if there was no small, true human being in whom thè truth would turn into joy and movement?

Voshchev would have consented to know nothing again and live without hope in the dim longing of vain mind, if only the girl were whole, ready for life, even if she'd suffer later in the course of time. Voshchev lifted Nastya in his arms, kissed her parted lips, and with the greed of happiness pressed her to him, finding more than he sought.

"Why did you bring the kolkhoz? I'm asking you a second time!" Zhachev spoke, without letting go either the cream or the pastries.

"The peasants want to register into the proletariat," said Voshchev.

"Let them register," Chiklin said from the ground. "Now the foundation pit will have to be dug still deeper and wider. Let every man from the barrack and the clay hut move into our house. Call all the government and Prushevsky here—I am going out to dig."

Chiklin took a crowbar and another spade and slowly went to the farthest end of the foundation pit. There he began once more to break open the motionless earth, because he could not cry, and he dug, unable to tire himself, till nightfall and all night, until he heard the bones creaking in his toiling body. Then he stopped and looked around. The kolkhoz followed him and dug the earth without stopping; all the poor and the middle peasants worked with such zeal of life as though they wanted to find salvation for themselves forever in the abyss of the foundation pit.

The horses did not stand idle either. The kolkhoz members rode them, carrying stone and rubble for lining the pit in their arms, and the bear lugged stones on foot, his maw gaping wide with the strain.

Zhachev alone took no part in anything and watched the digging labor with sad eyes.

"Why are you sitting there like an official?" Chiklin asked him, returning to the barrack. "You might at least be sharpening the spades!"

"I can't, Nikit, I don't believe in nothing now," Zhachev answered on that morning of the second day.

"Why, vermin?"

"Don't you see I am a cripple of imperialism? And communism is the children's business, that's why I loved Nastya. . . . I'll go now and kill Comrade Pashkin, as my parting deed."

And Zhachev crawled away into the city, never again returning to the foundation pit.

At midday Chiklin began to dig a special grave for Nastya. He dug it fifteen hours on end, to make it deep, so that no worm, no root, no warmth nor cold would ever reach it, and so the child would never be troubled by the noise of life from the surface of the earth. Chiklin carved the coffin bed in everlasting stone, and readied a special lid— a granite slab, so the enormous weight of her grave's soil would not oppress the girl.

After resting a while, Chiklin lifted Nastya in his arms and bore her carefully to place her in the rock and cover her with earth. It was night. The kolkhoz slept in the barrack. And only the bear, sensing the movement, awakened, and Chiklin let him touch Nastya in farewell.

EUROPEAN CLASSICS

❧

Honoré de Balzac
The Bureaucrats

Heinrich Böll
And Never Said a Word
End of a Mission
Irish Journal
The Train was on Time

Lydia Chukovskaya
Sofia Petrovna

Aleksandr Druzhinin
Polinka Saks · The Story of Aleksei Dmitrich

Konstantin Fedin
Cities and Years

Marek Hlasko
The Eighth Day of the Week

I. Grekova
The Ship of Widows

Ignacy Krasicki
The Adventures of Mr. Nicholas Wisdom

Karin Michaëlis
The Dangerous Age

Andrey Platonov
The Foundation Pit

Arthur Schnitzler
The Road to the Open